Author photo by   Nora McSweeney

Published in the United States by Fence Books
                                   New Library 320
                                   University at Albany
                                   1400 Washington Avenue
                                   Albany, NY 12222
                                   www.fencebooks.com

Book design by   Rebecca Wolff

Fence Books are distributed by   University Press of New England
                                   www.upne.com

Library of Congress Cataloguing in Publication Data
       McSweeney, Joyelle [1976–]
       Flet: A Novel/ Joyelle McSweeney

Library of Congress Control Number: 2007933973

ISBN 10: 1-934200-07-7
ISBN 13: 978-1-934200-07-0

FIRST EDITION

Excerpts from *Flet* have appeared or are forthcoming in *Caffeine Destiny, Cutbank, Fairy Tale Review, Fence,* and *Apocryphal Text.* The author is grateful to the editors of these journals.

The author would also like to express extreme gratitude to Kate Bernheimer for her help in the revision and assembly of this book, and to Rebecca Wolff and Johannes Göransson for their continued suggestions and feedback during the finalization of the manuscript.

 are published in partnership with

and

and with help from

A NOVEL

JOYELLE MCSWEENEY

ALBANY, NEW YORK

A NOVEL

CONTENTS

FLET 1

BEGINNING WITH THE INTRODUCTION AND CONVERSION OF FUEL

Driving away on wheels, the internal combustion. Driving away on pistons. Driving away on mica. Driving away on cliché. The rough road pitted as a line of type. Between coupes, eighteen wheelers, and transports: engines. And now alone, driving through the former fern-lands and arthritic trees humped up the sides of the road. And now slowly under fast-food emblems tuned in the sky to the frequency of daylight. Driving the neckline of a blouson sea the grey cliff is cupped to. Driving the guardrails of a chalky cliff that obliterates knowledge and will not subside. The white cliff marks the edge of knowledge, which is a knowledge that will not subside. The mind studies it, furling ahead of the barge from Nation B, or gazing back at it from the great falling-apart-of-thought that is the crossing over.

What's on the other side?

A mist or glare settling over Nation B.

What's—

You can't drive to the coastline. You can only drive so close to the white chalky cliff and then you have to get out and dive.

★

Flet is standing outside the car. Hyperfluorescents blaze from the enormous rectangular platform floating hundreds of feet over her head. The plinths that support it are erased by dark. The fueling pavilion is lit like a studio or an underwater mine set. Fuel is promising itself into the car. Jingles and messages fray from the screen above the pump. Flet leans her back against the broad curve of the side door and feels the moisture soak through her suit. She feels grit and grime seeping through.

On the postcard-size screen, a flight of wolves over a snowbank. Flet watches the image stutter as the credit card reader chokes down her information; the wolves retract and launch again over the snow, their silvery snouts long with inclination. They sink towards their blue shadow. When the foremost paw breaks the snow's surface, the footage speeds up. The wolves crash down in a tide of white powder. A double-bladed logo is released and springs up to take the place of the moon.

The pump clunks off angrily, the snow-scene cuts out, and off Flet goes, out of the elements (oxygen, moisture, other humans) otherwise endemic to life on this planet. She likes to be strapped in, her hand on what are still called "the dials," punching up different frequencies of static available in the darkness. For free: the static of deep sea. A parliament of whales in caucus. The thoughts rocks and corals drive through their skulls. This constant conversation is converted to display as constellations hidden behind the pink interface. These may be watched on filetape though rarely seen through the smudged troposphere, which looks more and more solid despite the many atmospheric holes. Tonight is greasy. She's out of range. She listens to the incomprehensible messages in the static. She drives until the road and sky are frighteningly indistinguishable and then she drives without fright.

METHODS OF CAPTIVATION

Can anything captivate these households? Brittle condos shingling the valley floor with artificial light, they keep a mysterious math. They are utterly divisible into point after point after point, yet work like clusters, their infinity unmatched by anything manmade on earth except the particles eating the sky. The Companies have figured out how to project logos onto rain-clouds, but not (yet) how to improve the weather, and not (yet) how to fit each drop with audiofiles. They settle for crude compromise: the lid of an effervescent fluid printed with an access code. Waved before a sensor, the code unwinds online into a hiccupping pop song. In a year or two this tech will seem as blocky as an Edsel or stale as a dispatch from Eden. So: what's captivating these households tonight?

1)The blood sports of extinct empires.
2) Oil reef economics.
3) A salute to the history of media salutes.
4) Soft-drinks, hair-dye.
5) Pictures of the weather.
> The weather roils by all day on this English Channel. It's rendered over in math, abstracted to beautiful contaminated blots and statistical clouds that interrupt the stream of pictures like a god or code breaking in to assert its superior reality. Rendered back into image, it plays in realtime on wind-whipped coastlines and remote ill-starred exurbs cratering into mud. Distressed survivors huddle illustratively or claw up cliffs or weep on overpasses dressed in neon, rain-soaked T-shirts screenprinted with the slogans of corporate sponsors: Product is life. Life is good. They need new pacemakers, peacemakers, mini-fridges, maxi-freezers, personal gaming devices, they've lost their PC cards and their pets. They need new hair-weaves, hemoglobin, blankets, and stents. Though

the structures have fallen, yea, the infrastructure hath remained. The mayor, retrieved, transmits from the ruins of his office.

Meanwhile, in a drier disaster, Child A has been fitted with a microchip under the skin of his right thigh so he can be rescued from the cactus forest where his baby blanket has stuck and shaded him from sunstroke, evidence that prayers are answered every day. His sister, Child B, has lost her leg and so unfortunately cannot be dug out in time from under a boulder in the dry arroyo. And Children C through Z^n have no microchips to speak of and so live and die uncounted on continents so far away from the home office that perspective shrinks them, even in the mind's would-be limitless eye.

Yes, the T-shirt is right. Life itself is good. It blooms like weather all over the earth and it goes out like a lamb and a light.

6) Filetape of Flet.

7) The Medicine Chest, formerly known as the Prescription Network, until Nation did away with doctors five years ago and let the Companies minister directly to the citizens.

8) The Heaven Network, cosponsored by the Medicine Chest, in which gold-hued seniors rake leaves and frolic in the buttermilky light.

★

Filetape of Flet:

Those tuned to Informed Electorate may see Flet. She is seated three rows back from the testifier, seems to float over the testifier's left shoulder. Flet's black suit and chestnut chignon frame neat, average features on her neat, average, oval face. Her eyes are a warm, unobjectionable brown behind her glasses. Her glasses are fake, and have been treated so as not to reflect the studio lights. She stares ahead with her mouth tightly closed. Three subtly manicured fingers are visible at the left edge of a brown clipboard, its steel clamp glinting occasionally under the brights.

Testifying today is Flet's boss. She speaks directly into the camera, she has a perfect knife-blade bob forming points around her chin, a mauve suit with a Chinese collar, a dazzling lotus-shaped brooch worked from a cluster of optical fibers. Her face is classically beautiful, regally aged, neatly made up, and, as she answers the questions she tilts her head slightly to one side. Periodically her brooch gives off a glittery signature.

As sub-secretary of education media, Lonnie Otis's job is to report, present, announce, endorse, decry, and, on churchdays, implore and praise. Flet's job is to accompany Secretary Otis to these screenings, clutching the antique clipboard that is the sceptre of her rank. She is not even sure where they found the clipboard, worries sometimes that it was retrieved from the sealed offices at Old Capitol, worries what antigens might be passing into her metacarpals and wrist bones and the steppes of her stomach as she wields its flimsy weight. She has plenty of time to think.

It's been years now since a party of influential parents used the imperative of the Emergency to successfully lobby for an entirely remote educational system. That a pressing need for Brickless schools existed before the Emergency was a matter of near consensus. For years beforehand, natural but toxic bacterial strains had accrued and been transmitted in the classrooms and cafeterias of the few remaining physical schools. That was to say nothing of the social and behavioral contagions creating rifts and dissent among schoolchildren in different localities and regions. The Emergency clarified vision, made it self-evident that any group of citizens was a potential target, and children the tenderest and most inviting target of all. A standardized Brickless curriculum would remove such threats and place Nation's children, its most precious though not its most numerous or remunerative resource, in accordance with one another and out of harm's way.

A horrific event in a nation so far across the world that its name could not be fixed in the minds of most citizens cemented in these same minds the need for immediate conversion to the Brickless system. In a secondary industrial city of this far-off nation, a party of gunwomen entered a primary school on the first day of the fall session. The children were too bowed down with flowers, chocolate, good luck trinkets, and heavy breakfasts to defend themselves. This happened in the shadow of a mountain considered sacred to several religions, which was subsequently partially exploded by one or another side as the government, aided by Nation's advisors, hunted the evildoers up into these holy elevations and there lost the trail amid heavily fragranced natural chambers.

Flet likes her job. She meets Secretary Otis at her house each evening before a screening. Secretary Otis pours thin intoxicating liquids into improbably teetering cups as Flet downloads the next day's scripts. Then Flet reads the entire script through while Secretary Otis listens. Next, Secretary Otis reads the Nation lines, and Flet reads back the responses Secretary Otis is expected to provide. Finally, Flet acts as Nation and Secretary Otis responds with the silvery, soothing lines which she will deliver the next day.

At sixty, Secretary Otis is a rising star in the Administration and a Company girl from way back. She was one of the first New Models, representing the liberated woman by donning a flimsy yellow nightgown and rippling through a field of daisies representing shampoo. As time passed, she became the image of female empowerment, driving larger and larger cars, confidently selecting diet pills, always returning to the shampoo and hair-dyes that allow each woman to control her image and her destiny. As education media secretary, she has been flawless, particularly good at churchdays and in adapting the script to the inevitable misreads and ad libs that occur at open venues. Her screenings draw small but perceptibly larger audiences than other cabinet members, and it seems only a matter of time before the Administration appoints her to more significant affairs.

But, for now, she is content to sit on her silver couch in her light purple robe, looking at her and Flet's shadows on the unlit filetape screen. Both she and Flet drink silently, meditatively. When her glass feels light in her hand, Flet rises from the couch and says good night to Secretary Otis. She steps out into the night air and pauses. This land used to be a fern forest, and modified ferns still line the doorstep and the driveway, minutely irrigated and bred to form protective waxes against the scorching sun. A floodlight douses them from the house, their electric green glowing overtime in the massive night.

6

★

Well-ell-ell
          Well-ell-ell
Ohh-oh-oh
          Ohh-oh-oh
Well
          Well!
Well
          Well!
Oh! Baby please don't go!

The drink worn off and the gas tank filled up, Flet drives into the nimbus of a radio signal filtering back to earth. A raspy, roomy call and response bounces from speaker to speaker around the car's interior—a few feet from her right ear, just under her left elbow. It pinches and fondles her. Baby please don't go! Flet isn't going anywhere, just spending down a few hours of the night and dutifully using up her monthly fuel quota. Now the tears fill her eyes: tired? She cries and laughs at herself as she sings along don't go—back to New Orleans! with the song she's not even sure how she knows. New Orleans, the History Channel, the murky city on the Delta, a moist, enormous swindle from hungover France to which slaves and gamblers drained and from which an antic music briefly fizzed and subsided. Nothing broadcast from there anymore, nor any of the other cities. She would definitely not be going back there, she assures the singer presently wailing in the fedback wall of sound.

Flet drives out of the narrow channel of reception, through her sentimentality, and feels the quieted, gathered dark like heavy fabric all around her. She can almost sense the arms and trunks of the ghost forest, the levered canopy and the stoma of the bony ferns closing on a former viscous night. She knows she's just imagining this; her true gift is inorganic, a sense of technological timing, ghosts and traces. A touch of her hand makes radios tune more precisely and filescreens race more nimbly over the vast porous catalog. The health associates assure her this effect is chemical; they compare it

7

to the way some people have gravitational fields so specific they can make wristwatches stop. If it troubles her, they say, she might be able to control it dietarily and certainly through a minutely customized pharmaceutical regime. But Flet has no desire to change this part of herself, the trait that has been with her through her lifetime's inexplicable, uncoordinated stages.

The road, though curved, descends through the angular flights and stepped terraces of the valley to the depth of her development. Christ, she mutters as the engine motor clucks out curbside. She throws her keys in her purse as she heaves herself out of the car, then has to fish them out again before the brown, nondescript door of her home. It opens effortfully. Her feet sink archaically into the carpet as she steps inside. Minutes later she collapses fully clothed atop her bed, feeling her body elide with its comfort. Christ.

FIRST ENVISIONING OF THE MISSING CITIES
(HERBACEOUS)

The missing cities grow taller and higher. They grow over the vat. They grow portable: they blow like living yeast. They spread out and take a breath. They build the strongest net in the world: spider webs. They build a grave-blue cotton in the joists and laddering. They build a planked floor that the dust silts through in lines. The lines form the blueprint for the second city. The second city: the plank city: the roof city: the sky city: the weather city: the tropocity: the atmocity: the core: the mantle: the bodice: the beeline: the instep: the torch-sweep: the hatband: the screw: the driving glove: the foil tip: the eel cast: the net haul: the polished angle: the chopstick: the dagger: the dendrite: the patch-and-stain: the cobwebbed brain. Modeled where the proteins formed a hummock and a site; sugaring the blood 'til it crystallized (crystal city); the baby sucked the cuts; the baby tasted greasy or sweet, depending on its alkali: sweaty with lucky neutrality. First it was a symptom, then a system in the bassinette: to mint and multiply, to cover the mutation. To print the communication in relief from cell to cell. A material crier on hoof beats. A ghost Reiter that swept up late for the massacre at the stoplights before the Rite-Aid. No, the city: the center: already crumbling away: already hard to perceive, macular, marked out in milestones and hot keys, levers in the code that flip the stalwart passengers onto the next logroll. All politics is logroll, all free beer for the city, ladled out around the stump speech. High as a blind knee. This passenger tall as a leg of beer, in his pre-beard, non-electable. Then bearded and electable. So this is the little ladle that saved the big wand. So this is the address on the back of the envelope which ground will save the war. His roman à clef is sweet to the taste and turns like a key in the ear: ta dum. It turns like a key in the back. It's a wind-up. It's the pitch. When wind clattered clean through the hole in his ear that's the end of the wind-up. You've lost the battle, now the war. Your bad ankle is about to get worse, despite your excellent angle. Off into the night on hoof beats, in women's clothing. The bad message wants to copy itself, someone will tell it. The city joins hands and spreads out in a circle, looking for the drowned. Its windowpane walls can't bear it, then it's cellophane, it has Hincty Cell Syndrome. Once it's gathered and crimped it won't hold the same information. The city corrodes, gapes in the walls. Everyone leaves their posts and spends time sipping in the outposts. Flet alone through the enjambments and ambuscades. Outside people, inside weather and exposure, the city is materials, mutating and corroding and becoming cyclical. Becoming self-sufficient.

A STIRRING

Stirring a spoon on a lax wrist through a microcosm of bobbing flotsam, chemicals, hormones, vitamins, gritty sugar and milk, Flet slumps like a child. It's a remembered pose, half-bored and half-defensive, though no one is with her in the plastic yellow kitchen. With her head propped on one elbow, Flet watches programs meant for children feed one into the next on the notebook-sized filescreen. A Petri dish filled with clear liquid becomes a fit but geriatric man whose close-cropped white hair has been slicked back over his ears. He is the picture of post-executive leisure in his spotless French blue sweater and paler blue collared shirt, and as he hunches over the shoulder of the sample child, his slacks pleat audibly. In the Petri dish, a cork speared with a sewing needle flails desperately for North. Eventually North is found. We are encouraged to try this at home, where a leaf decked with a needle will perform the same trick. The leaf is of interest to Flet: gently curved, subtly serrated to reveal a complement of slick and matte greens. It is the ideal leaf, North American from some fifty years ago, deciduous, backyard-growing. She wonders at the groomed, restricted universe in which this science operates. She wonders if this science would function with a less than ideal needle, a less than ideal leaf. Or, looking out her window, with no leaves at all. With tinder-dry needles of last chance pines.

Flet drops her cereal bowl in the sink, scoops up her bag and exits the apartment in one motion. She hears the heavy door clasp closed behind her and the fat fangs of the deadbolt swing into the lock. The sun is strong outside at 9AM. She's glutted with the stream of craft projects and science experiments she's somehow imbibed and her thinking is pleasantly squirrelly, balled up. She remembers classrooms, pinning green paper leaves to bulletin-board trunks with the common pins she was surprisingly entrusted with, tracing her hand to make turkeys and doves, balancing the globes of the snowman one on top of the other. Lessons in iconography that changed with the month. Deciduous education. Now as she fans out her keys with one hand she flashes shadow puppets at the sidewalk with the other. Rabbit, duck. She can't remember many others. Yet the sidewalk gives Flet back each signal crisply. They understand each other, though they have neglected to work out the code in advance.

In her car, she notices the nose of her cell phone blinking blandly but drives without enabling the communication systems, which have been latterly added to her retrieved, pre-Emergency sedan. She hates to feel her mind drain away into these devices, into the workday. She likes her imperfect, mnemonic vehicle. It steers so heavily, so nautically out of the lot.

A SPECTACLE IN MULTIPLE MARGINS

At Near Cliff, the air is white as a teeth cleaning. Greek noon, carefully scripted for the teleforum. High above the semicircular dais, huge, flexing screens are suspended from portable plinths. On these, paradoxically enlarged little children sign and sing. A message crawls up the LED screen of each plinth like a snake or rodent—Brickless Schools 5.0—and like an object lesson is returned to the base of the plinth to climb again. Ethereal playground harmonies emanate from ankle-high speakers and climb up to the visages of the children who mouth them. A neat molecule of virtual tangibility.

The problem with not having real children at the screening is that Secretary Otis and other officials have no idea at whom to beam their professional-grade smiles as the performance continues. Gazing upwards has been ruled out. Except on churchdays, members of the Administration must always look forward. The event is meant to be viewed whole, from a distance far enough back or up to accommodate this. Secretary Otis expertly guesses which camera feed is on and tracks her benevolence at this ultra-pupil.

It is this gift which has enabled her to succeed.

> Parents of the Nation, I am standing before you today with some of the founding members of the Brickless Schools movement, which has liberated the Nation's children from the inestimably perilous confines of the common school. By educating the child in the home from an Administration-approved and reasonably priced curriculum package, we can shield our children from the immorality, disease, violence, and unmonitored and corrosive teaching that had become the norm in our Nation's classrooms during the administrations

preceding the Emergency. I am pleased to announce the release of the Brickless Curriculum 5.0 edition, which renders all earlier curricula obsolete. . . .

Flet spends all day in the chill, inutile air of a production trailer many yards back from the set, watching the Secretary and her colleagues move through the various segments of the telecast on a series of screens. One camera is always on Secretary Otis and feeds her image into a boxy, taped-together monitor. Although equipment always reaches the production crew absolutely new, the techies cannot bear to let anything go untampered with, unretrofitted, unimproved. Their passions are a paradox, at once analog and digital, tool-based and hands-on. Studying them over the horizon of her styrofoam cup, Flet isn't sure whether the nostalgia is the crew's or her own. The bareness of the folding chair aches into the bone structure in her legs, a déjà vu. Whiling away the hours in some airless classroom. The moment has slipped free of time. It could exist in decadesful of instants. Before the Emergency. During.

Flet turns her attention to the image of her boss, growing, shrinking, clasping, standing in the small monitor. In the medium shots, Flet detects with interest what she has never seen in person: a little lacquered shield gone up in the Secretary's almost purple eyes, behind which she has absented herself. Flet wonders how the monitor has clarified this, as she watches it appear again and again in the frame, this flatness where a glint should be. It is not the closeness of the shot, she finally decides, but the removal of some dimension of the face upon its conversion to pixels that allows Flet to study it. There she reads:

> *. . . Brother! This heat reminds me of one hot afternoon that got later and later without night ever coming down. In those days, cities had a way of hoarding heat in all their surfaces and structures, fire-escapes, railings, parked cars, tar roofs, awnings, paint splintering off a storefront, anything, as if heat was a precious currency and not just another cast-off dropped down on us without anybody asking twice. This particular day, I was waiting outside a drugstore in a*

dark brown sedan. The brown vinyl interior threw heat all around the car. I thought it might melt, me with it. I wore a cotton sundress, mint green. I had my hair ironed absolutely straight and the dry ends tickled my upper arms and found their way into my armpits. The street was almost liquid with heat. Do you know what I mean? People walked by in groups, the younger the larger, some squatted against the brick wall of the drugstore looking for a few inches of shade; it was that hot. My date was inside making a phone call. It seemed he had been gone a long time. I had already memorized everything in the car and now could barely recognize my own reflection in the rearview, from looking at it so long. I opened the glove compartment just for something to do, and in it was an envelope with a slim stack of photos not quite enclosed. My date was in most of the pictures, clowning around with a young woman, sitting on some painted porch steps, holding a beer in one hand and a tiny baby in the crook of one arm. He looked so strong, the way his body strained against his shirt and slacks, two shades of the same light blue. The picture seemed very recent, light was at that green and yellow angle summer casts on the edges of the city, and the same light flowed between my date and his pretty wife. Wife. Though it was not the only conclusion, that's the word that lodged in my brain and the iciness of it balled in my skull and cooled me like a plumb line dropped down my spine. I touched the metal handle of the door and stepped away without closing it, dropping the photos in a clump on the seat. I moved quickly and stiffly through the strange neighborhood, which was a fairly dangerous thing to do. I had no carfare, and was wearing cheap canvas sandals I'd bought with a few weeks' savings. I was sixteen years old. I thought Okay, I had my head turned, but now I'm seeing straight. I kept the low sun and then the sunset on my left. It got dark slowly, without getting cooler, knots in my shoulder where the anger kept burning off. By the time I reached my neighborhood, my emotion was mostly spent, but in the glow of my bedroom lamp, I sat amazed by how far my anger had taken me. My sandals had worn bloody ruts in my feet and the material stuck to the cuts as I pulled them off and dropped them loudly into the wastepaper basket. My arm stung where the handle of my purse had been rocking against it. I emptied its contents onto

my bed and chucked it out too. Then I gingerly lifted the bedspreads,
cluttered with coins and gum-foil and mirrored cases, and slid inside to
sleep. My feet burned, but my eyes also burned. I couldn't keep them
shut. I lay in my bed strewn with streetlight. From then on I could see
in the dark.

When the teleforum is completed, Secretary Otis and her peers are removed to a closed, portable studio to summit on another topic. Meanwhile, the crew in Flet's trailer are working to edit and assemble the final version of the morning's event. By the end of the day, Flet's brain feels grainy as she steps down the flimsy stairs. Secretary Otis is remote when she emerges from the second conference and is ready to be driven home. As per her instructions, the limo has been running for a half hour before she climbs into it. Its interior is creamy and thick. Flet likes how it clicks shut, how it seals all around them. The journey to the Secretary's home is brief, and as they reach the house the pale stucco walls reflect the dusk that has finally settled down all around them. A lazy student, it has smudged but not entirely erased from the sky the figuratively innumerable, far and near stars.

SPECTACLE OF THE PRESENT MOMENT PERFORMED IN THE PAST

In the filetapes that scour the air above Nation are images of this moment's supposition. Futures that can only be hauled out and rendered visible through hyperbole, masks, sets, and props as overdone and flimsy as children's costumes. The future as hemicircular sunglasses that make the blind to see. The future as an angular hat. As a bubble wristwatch. The past as a flat, crownless hat, an inefficient means of carriage. The past as a hairstyle. Fuelless cars that float like saucers around a thoroughly urbanized future. God wears the universe like a bubble wristwatch. He's distracted in traffic, thinking about what to eat. He forgets about the weather. He forgets his passcode. He makes up for it with huge, barely fathomable clouts of intervention.

In the darkly sunny midnight of her yellow kitchen, Flet watches sex comedies about the cosmos conceived in her childhood, set in her present day. She remembers a grade-school visit to a museum. In the entrance hall, ships of all kinds hung from struts in the soaring, star-tainted ceiling: canoes, kayaks, galleys, schooners, rafts, yachts, catamarans, space capsules, as if all of humanity were engaged in some kind of race across the sky. Plaques at ground level identified the crafts and also the names given to the constellations by different civilizations: Sisters. Flint Boys. Grapes. Paintbrush. Hen-and-Chicks. General. Rainy Stars. Dry Stars. Clusters. Clusterers. The Market Place. The Gathering Place.

Such museums are now boarded and aging or razed on the shallow plazas of the crossed-off cities. In contrast to their cheerful literalism, Nation's filetapes form a model of human history too huge and erratic to be held in any one human mind, yet incorrigibly human-scaled in the units of its composition. New events are added all the time; others bounce back from some forgotten chunk of space debris. Some events are taped, retaped, edited, reversed, revised, time-lapsed, slowed, recreated, re-enacted, computer modeled, fictionalized, redacted, existing in a stalled frieze in file after file that only requires the contemplating eye to spring to life: Washington crossing the Delaware. A pink-suited Jackie Kennedy. Other events recorded in filetape never occurred at all, or occurred as gaps in the record having no interface on technological or literate time, no documentation more permanent than the rattle of the larynx, the flexing of the eardrum, a flash against the back wall of the eye, a fluttering of neurons at or below consciousness. These are missing from the record until some dreaming executive or ambitious community group recreates them and films them back into being. Such events take place in the represented aggregate, hooked by anachronistic stances and imprecisions of costume and dialect into any number of chronological or cultural categories. There is no longer any authoritative version.

Of all events represented in filetape, there is only one singularity: Emergency Day.

Emergency Day retains an eternal present tense, a series of events to be examined again and again in sequence. It is the one story that is not changed by repetition, that may be re-experienced, that is hardly a story. It is simply images. The footage begins with a camera trained on the Old Capitol steps and dome, beneath a hazy pill-white sky. There are no markers of time in this frame; it might be midafternoon, or midmorning. The marble dome and haze seem made of the same material, condensed to such density in the Capitol structure that it has sunk low on the screen. The bled-out flag of Nation flaps lustrelessly from the needle-thin pole at its crown.

What happens next takes place in the sky. Soundlessly, an insectoidal clot drops into view. The camera shot stays steady, but the viewer's own eye starts to copy the motion of this foreign body: down and across. The clot begins to morph, grows wings, now it has the form of an airplane, the flimsy, old-fashioned kind airplane-fanciers might stable, it seems to fly in quotation marks. From the top right of the screen, it drops low, then begins to climb up left, making its way out of the picture. Then, with such speed that the footage seems to jump a frame, two long, thin military jets materialize, hover before the eye, and are gone, nosing the kit plane off the screen as if by their very presence. The visage of the untroubled dome is restored, tomb-pale and calm.

After a minutes-long gap, garlands of white and grey multiflorous smoke waft separately from the left, begin to enwreathe and then scribble over the building, slowly filling the screen from the bottom to the top and blocking both sky and dome from view.

This is where the filetape ends, but the implications of E-Day depend on what is not shown, what is hidden in the smoke: a decoy bomb set off inside the Capitol; the members of both camerae of the deliberative body forgetting their training and rushing out into the toxic field of smoke. To become Martyr-Leaders, one and all. To be converted. To breathe, as the Brickless Civics script concludes, their last.

It takes eight minutes. Archimedes climbs out of the bathtub, finds a place to stand, wields his lever. Eight minutes later, he is scratching his backside in the tub. One insubstantial page is turned, one mote flicked away to make room for the next. There is time to contemplate and split this image, to see a million different pixels throng the screen. Mud and spit, current and ash, bone and trouble and bile. That's how the thrum of *then, then* gives way to an intense, almost endurable *since then,* the compound and accruing *now:*

NOW ARRIVING OVER AIRWAVES, AIRLINES

The black scarf knotted at her nape plots a green epidemic on her skull.
The black skiff skirts a knotty sea, a needle in mourning weeds, a razor-
edged reed, a toothed fish: a decision in motion. Not me yet. Whipping of
the foam of the sea: a fate or a fait accompli. Who wants to be drawn out.
Who would want to wear this crown. Poised on the crest, down in the flood,
rests in the pit, hurled up. Aurora dolorealis, spider writing, green vernal
ink, dawning branch. Scrawl from which I'll never rise up. I'm down now,
I lie in the graphite dust. Burning, the atmosphere snags and the child's
writing lights like a fuse. These are the Russian-made night-vision goggles
that were his eyes. These are the slick children's vitamins that reflect light
but don't produce it. Coin in the hand. Coin on the eye. Twist of bread.
Coin in the mouth. A child's braid. The wisps pull loose in the photo on
the grave. The milk-tooth in the clay. The skull glares back, drinks the day
into its channels of vision. A big-veined valley empties sightless amid the
hills of the hand. A future written in roods, routes, in roads on the bottom
of the lake. And now the future silts closed with dust from the bit-factory.
Wastewater shuttling with industrial gems. To drink it scrapes the throat: to
become raw and written on. It makes a surface inside. Cone of flowers in the
hand, untwisting. Stitch dropped. Rotting flowers sickling the halls, revolting
aptness. Hose it down. Everything drains away to become unreadable.
Somewhere the purest water lies where everything has come undone,
reduced past its separable elements. But not yet. Insufferable catalog: Nose
cone of the shuttle. Fishbones sunk in the rows to swim the spent soil
black. Choke fish turning mammal. Fin turning manual. Refuse fish. Man
turning mamma. Mad dog barking at her capsule-horizon, it comes back
constantly, hypofangs glinting with light thrown by the various satellites.
Thrones natural, manmade. Mother's milk, simulacrum. Saliva way, milk
way, lymph way, phlegm way. Filament way, lightbulb way, tinder way.
Cough and sleeve. Pillow slept. The humors of the universe. Pour them out

and sift them back. In the closed and continuing classroom, the brass brace holding up the earth. Soundproof windows. Crayon-shaded continents that fit the child's hand. Calm child sleeping between the lines of the lined paper. Between the red line and the blue line: pencil in hand. Plot the difference between the top of the letter and its tail. It makes a stuttery document to be measured but not read: the single letter stuttering across the page. Never on to the vowel, the heart of the word, which we supply in stereo, hurling it into the air, into the roots, into the stalks, into the knockoff microphones, the community boards, the sympathetic magic of peripheral democracy, wired to nothing. Only bouncing lightly off the satellites. The knife's glint, but not its edge. No one feels it. We enlace ourselves. Everything waits to be crowned or drains away. Heads and tails. We draw the pictures and burn them up. We drink and we bleed. The moon comes up. At the bottom of the channel/ the purest water/ lies. We don't believe it. We move back and forth, drive the warp through the grid, gird in fifth-rate nylons, the sweaters and shawls of manmade fiber, our lot. It must be worn out, or nothing destroys it. It neither burns nor breathes.

HOUSEWARES AS SECRET

Flet has a secret.

Wearing heavy blue vinyl kitchen gloves, she opens her hall closet, tips forward the hamper, and withdraws from behind it a paper bag. Kneeling, she dumps out the bag on the carpet next to her. The contents: a blue comb, a cheap Easter novelty, and a pale green pamphlet. The Easter novelty is a white plastic egg that stands on a base of blue basketball sneakers. Sprouting from the machine-cut crack at the crown of the egg are the tips of two pink rabbit ears; extending from each side of the egg are bits of fake-looking yellow feathers. In the unseen confines of the egg, is chicken becoming rabbit or rabbit becoming bird? Do they battle for the outcome, or enjoy a peaceful coexistence?

The egg and other items are artifacts Flet has found around her apartment, objects that somehow survived the neutralization team's sweep. At first she'd left each of them where she found them, at the back of drawers and closets, but now she keeps them together and draws them out every so often, always protected by her blue gloves. The comb, egg, and pamphlet are without value. They are junk. Neither risks nor clues.

The pamphlet is a simple green sheet folded in three, advertising some underfunded historical museum in Old Capitol; a sketch of a mouselike woman in a mob cap holding an outsized sewing needle graces the front. On the back is a square schematic map telling how to reach the museum from area highways. It is this map that interests Flet. Though she knows, of course, the general location of Old Capitol, it is on even post-Emergency maps, the roads to reach it are not. And who would want to reach it, deserted as it is, its façades and parks and flags saturated with toxic material of uncertain halflife.

It's Saturday. A curtain of white-blond light hangs heavily in the window. Flet stows the materials away and returns to her program on Nature. Both the program and the Nature are extinct, bouncing onto her filescreen from some barren rock in the universe or pocket of gas. The film itself seems drenched in pollen, the two white hosts yellowish in their uniform of stiff khaki shorts and blouses. Pythons and baby jaguars curl around their necks and limbs and seem grafted to them. The earth as a unit of grasses. Now the herd splits and reforms around the struts of a pipeline. The tall grass sweeps like sensors; the filetape begins leaping from program to program, producing a torrent of ibexes ilexes springbok roe deer brown bear antelope caribou whitetails reindeer ostriches lizards hares bullfrogs crickets puma wolverines wading birds creepers springers gliders monorails nightmares chincoteagues chinooks thoughtthrowers theoreticians beseechers torchraisers giftgivers bribetakers handclaspers potstirrers ribeaters banktellers teachers love.

Through the glare in her window, Flet makes out motion on the balcony opposite. Two small boys close in size, maybe twins, ride toward each other on matching tricycles. They move in slow motion due to the heat and lack of space, their heavy black heads leaning into each other like filetape of cells the moment before they split. It's a trick of perspective that brings Flet to her door. She steps out into the natural/unnatural heat. She closes her eyes. Her face in the sun, her vision is red with white angular plates shifting through it like cliffs seen from the sea. She feels a tightness in her chest, imagines waking up to find herself strapped down like Gulliver, little clones waving plastic toys at her from their chunky tricycles. In the distance, they're up to their necks in plastic Easter grass. Behind them, the harbor curves into view, puddled and silvery, a flexible surface.

DISCRETE EVENTS IN DISCRETE CHAMBERS

Night is dazzling and icy in the confines of this silver-lit banquet. Flet sits behind a railing one level up from the rink-like floor and tracks Secretary Otis as she moves through the hall. There are maybe one hundred people in this space. Only Administration members of the highest clearance are invited to such gatherings, or even permitted to attend events this large; the public itself is strongly discouraged from forming unauthorized large groups, thus making itself a target by numbers alone.

This is Secretary Otis's first invitation to an event of this caliber, and she is making the most of it. In her trademark weightless fiberoptic garment, she is almost literally a star wandering about the dark-light room. The black evening clothes of most of the guests are meant to evoke the night outside, but Flet thinks instead of the lightless mile of rock that separates this chamber from the floor of the valley.

Flet has chosen this location for its safe reserve from the action but now someone sits heavily down in the folding chair next to her. It's Mick from the editing trailer, looking typically underdressed in schoolboy khakis and a brown shapeless leather coat over his white shirt and dark grey tie covered in orange kanji characters.

"Flet, right?"

"Yes. Mick."

"That's right!" he says, smiling. "I didn't know you even noticed us in there. You keep to yourself."

"Just staying out of your way."

"Yeah, it's always a rush to get it together and ready for uplink," he says importantly.

"Mmm-hmm." She turns her body lightly away and back down towards the crowd, where Secretary Otis is engaged in a tête-à-tête at a draped table.

"Smart of you to dress her in the coat of lights like that. Easy to keep an eye on her."

Flet swings her jaw around fiercely and stares at Mick. "I don't dress her."

"Oh, what do you do then?"

"I'm her aide. We go over policy. I help her prep for the screenings."

"Oh. We'll both have our hands full next month, then."

"Next month?"

"With the E-Day Reenactment. It's a huge project, decisions have to be made by all the heads of the departments. Your Secretary is going to be the big star, representing the Administration on the ground. Tonight, the bosses on the media side are going to meet and discuss how the event should be taped, whether we should edit it together nice and slick or recreate the original parameters of the E-Day filetape, which are very 'tourist-with-tripod.' Complete simulacrum. Challenging! Um, am I boring you?"

"No."

"It's pretty important. The decisions are being made pretty high up. Most of Nation will either be there or be watching. We're pretty stoked. Where does the Secretary come down on this one? Multiple vantages or fixed shot?"

"I don't know."

"Oh, I get it." Mick grins again. "You know but you won't say."

Flet smiles. She doesn't want to betray how far from the decision-making process her boss really is. If Mick can't grasp how the system works, even from his position on the scene of most screenings, she's not going to point it out to him.

"Listen, Flet," he pauses. "I know I'm not the coolest cadet in the starfleet, but, do you want a drink?"

She does. With one last look over her shoulder for the flashing nimbus that is the Secretary, she follows Mick's dark form back from the railing, up a flight of stairs to a lit, ice-box of a sound-booth where a number of their peers and equivalents are perched on the chair-backs and the equipment, pouring harsh white liquids into plastic cups and smearing the reinforced glass with their fingerprints and chatter. Impromptu gatherings on or off duty are expressly against the rules. Flet wonders distantly if this small, concentrated square of flesh and light can be seen from the ballroom. Soon she is steadying a flimsy cup of spirits, smiling awkwardly. Someone hands her a papery capsule; following the lead of the others around her, she crushes it between her back teeth. A freezing gas leaps down her throat to her lungs and then expands, driving them open. Her chest, paradoxically, contracts. She is figuring out a way to breathe around her lungs when she feels a heaviness encircling her, looks up into Mick's face. Fine. She's happy to kiss him for a while, her chin scraping against his stiff-from-the-package shirt collar. Then his arms abruptly slacken; he steps back with a vague, concerned smile and wanders away, as stoned as she is. While things are still going relatively well, she wants to leave. She slips out the door, picks her way back to the observation deck, and watches the decision-making members of the Administration smear and coagulate in streaks against the floor, her boss a blinding, unincorporated light among them. She grips the freezing railing. The high is mercilessly steep but mercifully brief. It leaves a spidery headache that only worsens as Flet rejoins the Secretary and escorts her to the elevator for the long, vibrating ride to the surface.

WEATHERGIRL OF HISTORY: FLET CONVERTED TO A GAS

The weathergirl of history looks over her shoulder at the cameraman listing behind her. She keeps talking with a strained smile on her face, gesturing widely at the map which blinks out and on, intermittently emitting an electric wash of blue. "I'm sorry, there's a problem," she says uncertainly. "There's a . . . technical problem. But if you'll stay with me ladies and gentleman I'll be right back with your weekday forecast, with your workday—" and then, suddenly, the camera steadies. Someone has taken the camera arm from the grip of the ailing man. In the hyperfaithful exchange medium of the human gaze, Flet can read through the weathergirl's eyes the slumped body pulled from the room. Natural causes. Natural causes are what the weathergirl is all about. Then the kinks in her smile relieve, a bright, sunny roll of teeth emerges, and the weathergirl of history emits blithe promises of gusts and sunshine ahead, of a decisively changed weather pattern, and, as she says this, she turns her back just perceptibly on the viewer's childlike gaze.

When Flet sleeps she sinks into soundless black-brown chasms her body first goes box-shaped to fill. Then she is a chemical, sharp-edged gas seeping from a crack and collecting in a cloud at the top of a chamber. She peers porously, as if through a fine grain, many yards down at the lamps below her, which move in circular patterns at once as purposeful and random as ants. Worker ants, also the shape of thoughts trying to function collectively, apply to each other. She wants to move down closer, and with her freezing brain, she does, just feet at a time. Sinks, and swells, wrapping and unwrapping herself, until she recognizes the lamps as miners' helmets, and she feels so moved: humans! She sinks down to their shoulders their human hair and the straps of their overalls and the curves of their cheeks. They do not notice or respond. They continue breathing awkwardly out of their mouths, white eyes shining in the gritty darkness, pupils so huge and black as if to lead directly inwards to a second chambered space, reflective and infinite. Flet focuses into these, but in this direction the gaze is shielded, cannot be read. Looking away and down she sees space stretch out, the five or six feet to the cavern floor stretching hundreds of yards below her. At the very limits of her sight, the tools of the men sink into the rock, picks and drills and spikes and hammers. At contact, they give off puffs of powder or short-lived sparks. Sending a single breath up, Flet drains in closer. She wants a closer look at those sparks.

THE PRESENT MOMENT AS A DISTRIBUTION OF CHALK

Chalk dust hovers a solid foot above the crushed shell lot. Everything seems to hang in suspension here; even the low white building might be held up by the afternoon's thickness as much as held down by gravity or some other partiality to earth. Even breathing requires the labored selection of a particular breath from all possible breaths in the ether, bringing it close in to oneself like a blouse pulled down off the rack. Flet leans against the building. Surprisingly, the wall is quite cool, having been treated with a special heat-phobic coating, feels almost too cold, chemically cold against Flet's back. She pulls away, but the cold cast by the building's shell doesn't even project an arm's length. Unnatural cold.

The building is a dairy, as signaled by its milk-blue paint job, but might more properly be called a constitution facility, as milk is composed here from separate vitamin, preservative, and antibiotic ingredients. The dairy is the first of a number of stops Secretary Otis will make this week, for a unit on farm life to be included in the new Continuous Heritage curriculum package. The fact that there is not a single farm or dairy herd left in Nation, thanks to a series of leaping and cascading viruses that has rendered it economically unfeasible to grow, house, or even slaughter animals in proximity to one another, lends a certain challenge to this project. To edit together extant filetape seems insufficient; new material must be produced to justify each successive purchase. A slated think tank on newer, hardier lifeforms, including weedy hybrids, moebius-shaped bony fish, edible fungi and industrial bacteria, was deemed a PR timebomb and struck before producing any useful elementary-level songs or mnemonics. In the wake of that bungle, the Continuous Heritage Board, with oversight of all science programming, has insisted on a more traditional approach, and so, with help from computer animatrons, the littlest children are being taught to imitate a cacophony of barnyard noises, to tumble like the circus beasts or leap like the zoo monkeys they will never lay eyes on outside filetape. As members of preliterate cultures were able to memorize thousands of lines of epic poetry, so Nation's children have become a kind of arbitrary and impressionistic repository for those species most visibly and loudly absent from Nation's landmass.

Unfortunately, however, this particular dairy has been deemed not camera-friendly enough, with its white-on-white palette, its unassuming tanks and general lack of visual pizzazz, even given the ministrations of the animators. Secretary Otis is making her apologies to the staff inside, mollifying the drooping director. Flet is waiting in the white rectangular lot, absently grinding her right heel lower and lower into the pliant surface, the shells entering her shallow shoes and tickling the nyloned bridge of her foot. At a seemingly coordinated moment, the glass door above the concrete stair swings open, Secretary Otis steps into the glare, and long spindly rods extend from the corners of the building, spraying down the dusty lot with a milky grey fluid. Leaping out of the reach of the spray, Flet presses her damp body to the building's freezing flank.

THE PRESENT MOMENT AS A DISTRIBUTION OF CELLS

It is not news to Flet that Mick lives his life in a series of wire-lined labs, windowless studios, and editing trailers, always closed in one or another portable or inhospitable box. Even before the incident at the underground banquet, her natural workplace interaction with him has been set in one or another of these enclosures. Embodiment, on the other hand, comes less easily to him; enclosure in the human form with its organic shapes and unpredictable interfaces, especially as exacerbated by immersion in open, shifting air, is a matter of charming anxiety. Down the flimsily shallow trailer steps with a combination of exaggerated caution and haste which seems destined to ensure a fall, ambling rigidly across the lots and arid interstices of the requisitioned plant, he is clearly a man who wants to be back in his box, where conditions are controlled and his expertise demonstrable.

This Flet likes. It answers a call in herself, feels like the inversion of something at her interior which she knows the shape of well. This afternoon, having delivered Secretary Otis to her weekly meeting of the Progress Board, she crosses Mick's path as he is making for his terminal, bearing a thin plastic cup that is evidently melting into his hands.

"I see you, Flet!" he exclaims, his eyes in fact not leaving the meniscus of brown liquid leaping at the flimsy brim. In an instant he has crossed the courtyard, lurched up three stairs and is gone inside the densely tinted door. Flet peers after him for some moments, wondering if he is watching her through the reflective glass. She smiles despite herself, and when she notices the door move ever so slowly open a couple of inches, nudged by the tip of a scuffed brown shoe, she follows him inside.

★

"Things are very busy, Flet. Exceedingly," he emits, bouncing happily on his swivel chair, his eyes lit by the white lines of code sweeping the monitor. It crosses Flet's mind to wonder what besides coffee and cola keeps Mick and the other techies working late into the night. "We're here like, officially, all the time."

"And you would otherwise be?"

"At my apartment, duh. Or, maybe here. I'm working on my own thing, very confidentially. Okay, I'll tell you, it's a next-level chooser for filetape feed. Just a prototype, probably millions of nerds like me are working on something like this, as we speak. When I get it right, I'll probably just build some for my friends." He pauses, looking around the empty lab. "I could build one for you. For example."

"Perfect it first, maybe."

"Yeah. Yeah. Most people don't like you messing around with their filescreens. Even friends."

"Yeah."

"The problem is they haven't made all their decisions yet. For the Re-Enactment. So we have to simultaneously develop, this, like, array of attacks, and we won't know which to put in place until the very last moment."

"Oh?"

"Yeah. Totally awesome. It's like the army. Special Ops!" He turns back to the screen. Curiously, unending hours of labor, the product of which is certain to be abandoned, seem to feed Mick's energy rather than exhaust it. "Listen, do you have a few minutes?"

"Like twenty. Then I take the Secretary home."

"Okay, I want to show you something. It's supercool, but eerie." He opens a new portal on his screen and begins typing. A system of dark blue lines on a glowing field comes up. "So, these are the plans of this building, this very requisitioned Ford motor plant and corporate campus which we call home sweet work slash home."

Flet leans closer. Because her daily duties take her to a limited number of cells, meeting-rooms, megarooms and corridors, she has not been able to assemble a sense of the compound's size or layout in her head. Unprogrammed and off-the-clock exploring is not encouraged in Nation, particularly when on foot. But here's the whole compound, with annotated dead elements, a glass plant and a tire plant, coke ovens and blast furnaces, foundries and steel mills, the whole as difficult to fathom as the face of a remote planet, despite the fact that she is standing in its midst.

"Of course, most of this stuff is down to its foundations now, and we basically keep to this part, which was just offices for the muckety-mucks and venues for exhibits and stuff. But I guess there's this fountain court, closed off in this sector over here?"

"Uh-huh."

"Do you want to check it out? We can get to it entirely underground!"

Flet laughs, the secret of his attraction to this site now apparent. She follows Mick into the corridor and down a flight of stairs evidently intended for a maintenance crew at some earlier point in the building's history. They move through a series of shapeless and incidental spaces, among mostly silent metal machines, ducts, vents, closets, and lockers, all lit in a vernal emergency green. Finally they find the staircase they are looking for and climb up again, swinging open a gunmetal gray door and stepping into a brightly lit cell.

Flet looks up. Haze is sinking down from an opening in the roof the exact size of the square, shallow, empty pool that lies below it. On the floor of the pool, thick black cracks star out like punched eyes from the sunken nozzles. A green-tiled Greek key runs all around the inner wall of the pool. Sprays of weeds spring up in generous sheaves at random intervals. It takes Flet a moment to realize that three of the walls, recessed in shadow, are covered in figures, larger-than-life human figures in overalls and glittering helmets or with bright locks tied up in rags, standing watch with no expression in their dark and smoky eyes. The musculature of their limbs and chests, the terrain of their faces has been elaborately worked in different shades of tile, until the workers themselves seem like hewn or manufactured things. In their oversized hands they wield the totems of their offices, wrenches and mallets, welding torches and helmets, or reach forward to offer, as in benediction, a nut or bolt resting on a serenely glowing palm.

The fourth wall enfigures a rosy, benevolent explosion. Loving curvilinear pink and balmy swirls embroidered with gold motion lines pillow down from a gold pyramid floating like money in an upper corner. Rafting like a toy in this current, a green-and-gold automobile with gleaming chassis, yellow spokes and a knife-bright, glittering grill coasts downward, foreshortening suggesting that this gift of the gods will in a few moments roll fully formed out of the picture plane and into the court.

In the heyday of the fountains, the heights of the water might have blocked the sightlines from one wall to another, might have kept the mosaic figures from looking on each other or on the strange apparition of this car descending from above. But without the grid of abstracting water, two sets of workers now are gazing, eternally, into the channels of each others' eyes, while the third watches as the product of their labor glides down from heaven on an improbable nimbus without a trace of the brains or hands that built it and brought it into its machine-life.

When Flet turns back to Mick, he is hunched away from her, blocking something he is holding with his body. Stepping closer, she sees that it is her own cell phone he is hunched over. He is programming his number into her phone.

A WHIRRING

That evening in her close kitchen, watching frozen air curl and uncurl in tongues from the dry, mold-like frost coating the empty mouth of the freezer compartment, she has the urge to break apart, divide, race off in thousands of smart molecular pieces. To hold every piece of herself in herself; to rev, both key and engine, every part an interface that meets the surface. Meanwhile her own body feels remote as the flat greenish light filling the box of the refrigerator, resting evenly on its shelves and molded crevices. She hums. The light hums. She shuts the door. The light shuts up. Her white bag sits on the linoleum, bulging with work-related detritus, and when she hooks a wrist in the vinyl straps her flip phone tumbles out. She holds its scarab body in her palm and turns it 'round and 'round. Then she opens it and sees there, as the screen lights up, the frozen image of a woman turned not quite entirely away, her head attending in the other direction, her shoulder one motion behind, her ponytail caught lankly on the far shoulder of her lemon-yellow jacket, enwrapping her like a motion line. It's she, her body, stilled in this image. The instant splits and stutters before Flet realizes that Mick must have snapped the photo when he got hold of her phone earlier today. Her wrist flicks quick as a serpent's tongue; it brings up his number and his phone is ringing before she knows why.

"Flet!"

"You took my picture, Mick."

"Yes, but with your own phone."

"Even weirder."

"Well there it is. I confess to everything. Now what?"

"I don't know."

"Why'd you call?"

"I don't know."

"Your timing is exemplary because we're being driven out of the pod, can you believe it? Some kind of fumigation, apparently, and we have to clear out for a few hours. I'm like, homeless!"

"Are you inviting yourself over, Mick?"

"I think you just invited me over."

"All right, come over. I'm too tired to say no."

An hour later he is balancing on the impossibly large, hot, corduroy couch shipwrecked in Flet's living room. He holds himself like an impersonation. Flet slouches against the wall opposite.

"I'm keeping all kinds of comments to myself," he says.

"Thank you," says Flet.

"Such as, this place is a perfect relic. Pre E-Day, pre-filescreen even?"

"Mmhhm."

"Second comment: . . ."

"Aren't you going to keep any for yourself?"

" . . . I can't tell anything about you from this place. No gaming devices, no DVD release posters, no pinup calendars, no Disney figurines, nothing here that didn't come with the place. Even your filescreen is all hidden away. It's like you might not even exist when no one's around. Like you're a hologram? Or with the CIA. A hologram working for the CIA!"

"It's in the kitchen."

"Evidence of your existence?"

"Filescreen."

"Okay, Agent Flet. Don't you even, like, collect anything? My friend has this complete set of Hyperenhanced Silicon Rangers, including the very sexy chick character, and they were worth a little money before E-Day, but they're worth even more since then, since the cities went off-line, and the supply is locked up out there. He says he's going to go scavenging in Old Capitol for more but, like I believe that. They're not worth enough to go scrolling in the contamination-dome. Strolling. Or bring some kind of weird skin-eating bug back to eat everybody's faces. Or get totally arrested and put in some labor camp, writing lines of code for the rest of your life. Without a face."

"Could that really happen?"

"Trust me, it could happen. They have to grease up the inside of this mask, but you could live. It's scary, what's out there. What could be. We can't even tell. How long have you been living here?"

"A couple months. But it was properly decontaminated, before I moved in. I have the certificate. If you're feeling nervous."

"I'm nervous around you, believe me, all the time. Because you're pretty?"

This interrogative compliment makes Flet blush.

"I'm going to get off the couch now?"

Flet nods and meets Mick in the middle of the carpet. They kiss, then cant like two clocks meeting six hours apart. They kiss again. Mick steps back holding her hand awkwardly.

"How old are we?" Flet asks, embarrassed at her embarrassment.

"I'm twelve, emotionally, max. But that's eighty-four in dog years. Or only one four-hundred-and-seventy-seventh the halflife of carbon-14 . . . Compared to carbon-14 I'm very immature. . . . "

"I actually do have a sort of collection, here. If you want to see it"

Flet leads a grinning Mick to the hall closet, reaches behind the laundry hamper and pulls out the folded paper bag. She thinks briefly of her blue vinyl gloves, hanging over the sink in the kitchen, then opens the bag barehanded and dumps its contents on the uncertain-hued carpet. The comb sinks in its teeth, the plastic egg rolls to one side and back, and she has to shake the bag again before the pamphlet will flutter out.

"And this looks like junk but really it's—" Mick prompts.

"No, it's junk."

"Oh."

"But, it's junk that shouldn't be here. That the decontaminators left behind. I found it around the place, and sometimes I take it out and look at this stuff, and it looks so strange to me, like a word you say over and over. This egg, what is it, even?"

"Uhm, something that could kill us?" Mick is backing away toward the linoleum lip of the kitchen.

"Well, it hasn't yet. We're nowhere near Old Capitol. Why should everything from before E-Day be off-limits?"

"It doesn't have to be off-limits, it just has to be decontaminated, and you know this stuff wasn't, so why take the risk?" Mick sounds impatient from halfway down the hall. "Look, Flet, I need to get back to the pod. The fumigators should be outta there by now."

Flet gets up and goes to the kitchen, where Mick is at the door. "You're really leaving?" She realizes she is holding the green pamphlet in her bare hand, which fact shocks her, wakes up the air in the room. She feels wired, wags the paper at him. "You don't want to borrow my map?"

Mick laughs indeterminately. "You really should be careful with that stuff, and you know it, Flet. I'm sure it's no big deal, but still. I'll see you back at the ranch."

"This is the ranch. My ranch."

"Okay, okay, then I'll see you at the shop," he says. Then he slips off his hide-like brown leather jacket before stepping out into the heat of the night.

Flet is alone in her yellow kitchen, where the air is charged and curious, whirring all around her extinct map.

THE PRESENT MOMENT AS A SYRUP, AS A DYSTENDED SWARM

Synthetic honey is delicious, and because the people of Nation will pay to consume it, it is concocted with gusto. It tastes like continuity, ancient, angular Egyptians stirring their arms like ladles in the viscous lock, a berry basket floating by. Stout Sumerians working honey into their beer. Imperial honey: confectionary jade and gold-plated garments. Post-imperial honey: the pileated workers' caps, the strong arms outstretched, the broad palms up. Honey in every pot.

The honey factory is the same blue-white as the milk factory, in fact looks quite like it inside and out, so for the tour a scant handful of workers have knotted black-and-yellow striped scarves around their necks, the ends tucked neatly into their lab coats. The factory does, in fact, hum softly, though Flet can't tell if this noise is the product of the nozzles, baths, belts, and chutes nursing the product to fruition or if the steady racket is being pumped in through the comb-like speakers pegged to the corners of the walls. She is told before the cameras roll that she must keep to the white rubber path, that touching or leaning up against the metal walls may result in a sizable shock.

As the manager leads them through the several chambers, Secretary Otis smiles, points inquisitively toward each snaky apparatus, nods at the empty air at her elbow where an Education Media spokescartoon will later be edited in. In her dark purple suit, she looks like an amethyst in a water glass.

A set of ceremonial stairs is wheeled into the final hall and locked into place where a grey, tintless river flows under a plastic bridge fitted with nozzles and furls out the other side a florid gold. Secretary Otis climbs these stairs in take after take, surprised at the sight of the finished product sailing by beneath. She and the manager and the empty space beam down at the colorized honey, which rolls glossily in its white channel with only a hint of greyness showing where it laps the edges.

★

Back at the ranch, Flet stirs the ribbon-yellow substance into two low tumblers of whiskey and ice. How neatly everything folds into everything else.

Is whiskey synthetic?

"Everything's synthetic, Flet. Everything's made by something. In a manner of speaking, even honey made by honeybees was synthetic. You couldn't find a much clearer example of factory-style production than that." Taking the glass from Flet, Secretary Otis fiddles with the filescreen control. In an instant, images whir from left to right, a bolt of black, green, and gold. The stream stops on a scene of white children horsing around in a green yard and exclaiming in German. Their clothing and haircuts suggest the late nineteen-seventies. A cartoon figure, half-bumblebee, half-zebra, canters across the bottom of the screen and then flies sweetly into the distance on bees' wings. The ad appears to be for Band-Aids. The Secretary taps the controls, and here is a sunburnt man smiling at the camera through a long acute triangle of bee-beard. Deep broad leaves reach into the picture to tussle the man's sandy hair. The bees are as thick as sinners climbing up to God in fence-post paintings of Judgment Day. The next file shows human forms draped from head to foot in white dusters, grey-white gloves, and broad white hats trimmed with netting reaching down past their shoulders. Secretary Otis slows the feed way down, and she and Flet watch a purposeful ballet unfold; subtle, given the wholly draped forms. They sway, bend, tilt, hunch, turn the crowns of their hats towards the cameras.

The chooser skips. An elderly ingénue steadies on a stem before stills of her own youthful image. Her gauze gown inflorates around her white birdlike head and her famous jeweled eyes cast light. Above, her multiplied image furls like so many petals: kissing, swooning, dancing, driving, pouting under hair teased thick as gold plate. As the host's voice elaborates, this pioneer dedicated her life to improving the human eye's ability to consume depth off a flat surface: a soupçon, a soup plate, an impossible waist, a labyrinthine kiss, a tryst.

Blip. A boring soap-white shuttle locks into the dock. A glamorous lint-grey cruise ship slips into the slip. The vertical channel between buildings is filled with a queer bulging hull. A glass bottle broken on its belly reassembles like a gift in the beauty queen's dove-gloved hand. Her hair is twisted in two horns. *How did I get here?* she semaphores in grey-and-white gestures to the ministering crowd. No flag rises in response. Gritty sun stutters, the scene cuts off. A thick husk of fruit bangs down to the flagstones to spill a ruby labor of pips. We must labor to be pitiful, the motet grins. Suited torsos and clip mics rest thoughtfully around a table in the dark. The interview concluded, they are waiting for the cameras to shut off, but have instead been preserved in this non-moment. A model ties her hair into slick, ropy knots: strength. A crocodile twists between her bony legs: dry. That weed is really making me sneeze, that sunburn really burns me. Cry. Repeat. Recap: Animated ants eat Day-Glo grains in time lapse, become a super-race, build a desert community of golf courses, ranch houses, exochurches and endoschools. A community in its own image, with its own sustainable carapace. It can drink through its own skin: big problem. In no time at all a rundown from a chemical peak flummoxes the race.

Slender evening wanes into thin, late nite: a window creases, goose downs, glass gone wet with heat deposits its roll of sand all at once. Seven centuries in one blow. Cave of sleepers. Cathedrals slump. A buddha gives way in a shudder of dust. A crowd of widows wails on a muddy bank above a fast-moving dark brown river. Records revolve. A flock confuses and falls. Titles resolve. Full skirts at the malt shop fly up: the rage. Count the elbows a phone booth. Fists pounding on the juke box. Make the record skip. A single malt. A single shot. A dizzy trajectory. A shooter. A spree. A frisbee. A burst. A thready clot. A single engine plane drops like an insect through a narrow chute. It drops towards a marble dome low in the frame as a hat-crown or a cake.

Emergency Day.

The ice clinks in Secretary Otis's drink as she sucks a breath. No matter how many times they see this footage, she and Flet always watch it through to its end. The inevitable shark-grey jets emerge simultaneously, nose the black clot off the screen. The thready garlands sweep in from the right and begin to wreathe the building. Soon they conceal Old Capitol entirely from view. Behind the dove-glove-colored smoke, the Martyr-Leaders are running. To their deaths.

Flet starts to say something about the upcoming Reenactment but stops with a syllable hanging in her mouth. Because now, for the first time ever, the screen does not freeze when filled to opacity. Now, for the first time, they watch the smoke slowly separate; over some minutes, it entirely clears. The dull sky is restored, then the spindly flagstaff, and then the hemicircle of the dome comes into view.

Then the body of the Capitol, its plaza and steps, with no men's forms clumped or contorted in the attitudes of their final demise. No array of decimated congressmen.

Flet and the Secretary sit bolt upright on the couch. It is as if their thoughts are made of ether, burning off as they leap from one skull to the other, too quickly to be converted or verbalized. They see a bird drop into the frame and swim off. They see many minutes pass while the flag flips restlessly in the breeze. The sky begins to shade a strange, cocktaily color of peach and pink. Then, a stirring in the deep center of the frame. A dark cluster emerges, which some moments reveal to be a group of people, colleagues, a senator and his staff. They move down the many flights of steps in a casual chevron formation, chatting as they go, firming up the strategy for tomorrow. At the bottom of the scene, they part ways and stroll out of view. Another cluster emerges in the screen above them and descends the steps.

Flet and the Secretary watch in silence as one by one the Martyr-Leaders leave the building, perfectly alive.

AN OIL DREAM

The Secretary in a nimbus, a caul. Before a glittering wall, under the pinpoint spot. Sugarplum Frost. Mulled Wine. Autumn Leaf. Fresh Grape. The names pressed on bullet-sized canisters stacked behind a sheer acrylic plate. Skate Blade. Ice Princess. Cobweb. Bandolier. She glimmers and twists in a glare like a ribbon that pulls tight and belts around her. She ducks, bobs, weaves, throws her chin at its best angle, winks one eye, pivots on clear plastic heels. Her bland trench coat unbelts. She cuffs it up, shrugs it off. Beneath it, a slip in the color called nude, lighter than her own skin. Her skin shines more brightly than the satin. She turns one shoulder. Another shoulder. Her lips: Plum Cup. Schoolhouse. First Blush. Sunburn.

Around her, cardboard female heads with jewels for eyes rise like sea-snakes among the glittery stacked displays, gleaming under layers of laminate. The jeweled eye represents: desire. For: makeup. Secondarily: money, men. They hawk a product called Brilliant, Happy.

The spot snaps out. The store is lit by security bulbs at the four corners. The dimmish light recalls a closed, smoke-lit room. A tomb. Who would be packed off with these goods to the afterlife. Rows of powders, shadow, eyepencils, lipsticks, lipliners, lip glosses, hair straighteners, hair removers, hair restorers, hot combs, flat irons, curlers, wands and picks, petroleum converted into form after form, sealed in thin and thinner plastic. The locked case of perfumes in breakable flasks: a classic offering. Old shampoos in new bottles.

The Secretary stays away from the shampoo aisle, her old province, where she once ruled barefoot, a loose-robed, clean-limbed girl. With the spot off, she loses interest in display. In the dark, she seems bigger. It is not clear where she ends. She runs one dim finger over the metallic inventory control gates that guard the entrance. The blueblack landscape is pressed flat beneath the glass doors. A red light on a hilltop blinks on and off.

In a back corner of the store, Flet appears insect-small, then doll-small in the belled security mirror. She wears an antique chocolate-colored beret retrieved from the Secretary's closet. She wears her coat belted closed. She appears to be studying the white grating rising from the pharmacy counter, like a gate to some florid resort. She turns and walks down the store's central aisle, her head turning slowly to either side. Abruptly, she turns in and is obscured by stacked product. She returns to the pharmacy counter, walks around to the side, appears in a second mirror kneeling and fiddling with its lock. Who is here to catch these sightlines? The Secretary enters the frame and stands at her shoulder. They both disappear and appear behind the grating, staring at the shelves of suspensions, spills, and tinctures. They have retrieved shopping baskets and hold one under each arm. They sweep into the plastic baskets salves for delay and indecision, panic and heartstop.

Isn't it all like a movie, the Secretary breathes, and her breathing fills the air.

Or

What would your dream-life be.

Yes. This.

★

As the image of the emptied Capitol gives way to a loud, plastic-hued ad for breakfast at a long defunct fast-food chain, Secretary Otis grabs at the controls. She tries to get the choosing mechanism to reverse, but her blunt ministrations only cause the images on the screen to leap further and further away from the E-Day footage. Flet retrieves the filetape log from the evening's feed and runs the codes again, but this time when they arrive at the E-Day filetape it elapses just as the women have always known it, with the enwreathed Capitol dome disappearing from sight. The smoke never clears, and then it freezes: The End. They watch it go white again and again, as if trying to scrub their brains white, or trying to scrub from whatever cranial cul-de-sac or kernel of the brain the unthinkable image of the Martyr-Leaders' survival. But that image remains as vividly as anything on the screen: in the mind's eye, the men stride banally and profoundly in their grey suits into the changing evening. They are burnt into every new scene the filescreen provides, burnt into the mysteries of the sea-deep, sauntering down corals and clambering across the anemone's ridged back. They emerge and part within the confusion of green-hued soldiers prosecuting some twentieth-century war. They emerge from a space-rock, a bedsheet, a blackboard: They do not die.

On E-Day, when the heretofore faltering Administration had roared awake and, jamming the filescreens with footage, reinvented the Nation as a state of permanent Emergency, the Martyr-Leaders did not die.

PLOT AS A TOPOLOGY OF HYDROSTATIC PRESSURES

Flet slides her right thumb over the sweating, knuckled surface of her glass, which held a finger of rum and a fist of advertised soda, which delivered the initial bite and regarding swoon of imperialism, which, full, settled down so correctly into her hand, which empty is a lack that raises it up: tumbler. Cartesian diver.

"Who, me?" she asks. Rita Hayworth.

"Flet." Secretary Otis is standing over her. Her powdery makeup looks as if it has slipped a fraction of a centimeter down her face, so that it does not quite synch with her features.

"Flet, the sun's coming up. It's morning. We haven't downloaded the scripts, let alone run through them. I'm going to get in the shower and you are going to make us some coffee. And then we are going to decide what to do."

Flet lifts herself up and walks effortfully over to the smoked glass cabinets of the kitchenette. She tries to shake her fatigue and mild drunkenness from her temples. Holding the edge of the almond-colored counter with both hands, she feels as if she is grasping at her own forearm, pushing against herself to stand up. She is curious to see the sharp edge of the counter rushing towards her, and to hear the metallic jolt of the silverware drawer beneath it as she bangs her forehead on her way down.

Secretary Otis runs in slippery from the shower, hauls Flet up and sits her at the little table, which cannot hold her upright, feels like the idea of a chair and table. The Secretary wrenches ice from the freezer, clunks it into a hand-towel, and props Flet's bent arm, hand holding this bundle, against her forehead.

"Keep it like that." She hurries back toward the still-running shower. She returns to a Flet awake and dazed.

"Are you that drunk?" The Secretary asks.

"No," Flet answers dully. "Hungry."

"There's nothing in the house," Secretary Otis snaps, getting up to rummage in cabinets, finding two canisters that heat their contents when the lid is twisted. Inside, a plastic-tasting soup.

"I had a dream, about E-day." Flet stops and meets Secretary Otis's eyes through twin plumes of steam rising from their open canisters. Secretary Otis is staring at her levelly. She has lined her eyes but wears no other makeup yet.

"A dream about E-day?" Secretary Otis asks evenly, as if reciting.

"I saw it. We saw it together."

"We saw it together," Secretary Otis pauses for emphasis, "in your dream."

"No," Flet begins, at first thinking that she isn't being clear, and then realizing that the Secretary is not asking but correcting her.

"You had a dream that we were watching filetape of E-day together. And?"

"And the Martyr-Leaders. Weren't—"

"Flet," Secretary Otis begins sternly. "You had a dream. Dreams are wish-fulfillment. We all wish this nightmare would be over, but it isn't. It's real. No doubt this talk of a Re-Enactment has confused things in your head. And I must say this plainly: You had too much to drink last night. I'm disappointed in you."

Flet is listening so intently to Secretary Otis that she isn't listening at all, the words sinking down around her as she focuses on the strange channels of the Secretary's eyes. how her hair hangs limp and wet in coils and drips on her elaborately pleated collar. Pattern on pattern. Measures of time.

Flet clears her throat. "You have a taping at eleven."

A knot pulls tight in Secretary Otis's eye. "I'll handle it. You, Flet, are taking the day off."

Flet feels something diverge within herself and pulls a breath in to fill the space. She stands up, famished, drawn to her own vanishing point:

"Secretary Otis, we both saw it."

"I don't want to hear anything more about this dream," Secretary Otis answers, not looking at her. Then she does look up. "And Flet. I'm saying this in all kindness and sympathy and I sincerely hope that you will take it that way: Don't bore other people with your dreams."

Flet steps out into a blinding morning. In her jacket pocket, the crumpled record of the night's filetape feed.

A FLYING

Flet is flying on the Great Deciduous Plateau. Few trees are left here, but the earth itself is somewhat deciduous, rising and falling away to an angular rhythm. Here and there, run-off carves odd, soapy-looking characters in the dirt. Florid survivor-flowers that thrive in the exhaust-blanket wave with lobotomized cheer from the median strip. They look like poppies, probably modified. The guardrails run on like faded ribbon.

The guardrails run on like faded ribbon, like an unbroken thought, a single slate-grey condition. Last year eighty percent of Nation's guardrails were fitted with intelligent strips that could register whose hands had touched them, whose breath had elapsed near them, or so the Administration had announced. Looking out at this gently warped and dusty-looking material running on for miles, Flet wonders for the first time if it's true. If anything is true. If everything is true. Could the sensors hold up under all this heat? Isn't this the same unadulterated, saggy-looking material that has always run in her periphery, from her earliest, unplaceable memory of riding, her cheek against the pedestal lock, her fat legs burning on the dark blue vinyl seats?

On the other side of the highway, citizens speed along behind shields of solid light.

Occasionally she passes a subdivision, and a dried-mud colored sound barrier rises up on both sides of the highway. Its flat plain reminds her of the filescreen at Secretary Otis's house, the Martyr-Leaders strolling down into the plaza and off into the mundane night.

When she has covered enough rushing distance, Flet is ready to think this out.

It is possible that what they saw is nothing exceptional: two pieces of filetape run together by accident, or even intentionally by the chooser's logarithm. First, E-Day, and then, unrelated, a prior shot of the Martyr-Leaders exiting the Capitol.

It's possible that the footage is some kind of fraud deliberately planted in the filetape feed to sow doubt among the citizens of Nation. In that case, it is necessary to report and denounce it. In that case, they must act immediately, even a night's passage begins to be suspicious. And yet Secretary Otis has sent her away for the day, has decided that the best course is to deny the filetape's existence.

As she attempts to poke her way through this netted series of thoughts, another iron-colored thread knots around her: Who could know they have seen it? Who out there was watching the log?

The matter of a Nationwide, coordinated filetape log has been vexing the Administration for some time. On the one hand, they've hired thousands of retirees and stay-at-home mothers to monitor and analyze phone and filetape logs by sector, plus upload security and traffic tapes generated by the cameras like the one under which Flet is now passing. Secretary Otis was featured in a brief spot explaining the program, standing shin-deep among the survivor flowers, pointing at the flimsy insectoid camera clamped high above the highway. Vigilance, she smiled, keeps us Still the Nation. But the problem with this vast system, as with the highway tape, is that it is too large to be functionally preventative. It can only work in retrospect, moving backwards towards an initial aberration. It only works if you know what you are looking for.

Finally, Flet considers the most upsetting possibility of all: that last night's filetape records some kind of truth.

Truth. Could the medium even bear it? Amid all the ads, reruns, cartoons, re-enactments, fiction after celluloid fiction, stunt performances, telethons, addresses, and events? In this context, what did this filetape matter? Why give any weight to it at all?;

Flet thinks as she threads the needle of the horizon and begins dropping down to her development,

why give any weight to it at all.

HELICAL INDICES

In her apartment at midmorning, darkness and light settle out of each other like oil and water. Flet showers, the blandness of the yellow-brown tiles comforting to her, water beading up on them as in all showers, everywhere, chlorine fumes swirling in the steam. She is one of a million citizens of Nation showering at this moment, Flet thinks, and then grimaces to catch herself thinking in Administration-speak. The matte shower curtain stains the light with the same hue, this frankly ugly color grandiosely titled Harvest Gold. She parts her hair in the mirror and combs the tangles out, and she likes how her hair separates as it dries, curling around itself, helixing; by the time it dries it's straight. She looks at her body, which is growing heavy in places, though her clothes hide it. She is getting older now, without even thinking about it. Is her body the record of a past lived or of a growing forward in time.

She smoothes flat the printout on her kitchen table, its vinyl coating like cartoon wood. Her filescreen is simpler than the Secretary's, and she does not have a device that will let her enter back in the serial numbers printed minutely in green ink. But she studies the numbers anyway, her fingertips on the controller. The first set of numbers is for bees. She keeps her eyes on the code like an incantation, and when she looks up bees fill the notebook-sized screen as if it is a window into a hive. Black-and-gold bodies, brown tinny wings, a brainlike activity when taken as a whole. They stream down the screen like gold or money. These are the workers; elsewhere are the queen and servants, nurses, handmaidens, drones but no king to choose among them. Somehow the choices are already made, coded into them, they've been fed on clotted or diluted admixtures and jellies that bring their natures to light. Now the screen is filled with pen and ink sketches of Greek maidens, white as columns.

She taps on Sound and catches the commentary. The bee-girls, the honey-colored gowns, the bear-dance, the destruction of the hive to harvest it, the smoked tunnels, frames, and skeps. The bees return. With one finger on the paper and the other on the sensor, she watches the screen image swirl from the heaving hive to widows on the water, frolicking cotton-clad children, the bee-man's sleuth-y, slithery beard. She takes her finger away. A caravan of men escort a white-clad white woman to the mouth of a system of caves. A diademed elephant kneels. A white embryonic beluga threads what seems to be a city river, under a clacking, rusty collection of pipes, fences, belts, and ramps.

And then the dome at Old Capitol, the hazy day, the handful of airplanes, the billow of smoke. Flet stops breathing, willing the clouds, once again, to clear. But the screen freezes in fog.

CITY AS A MAXIMUM FIELD OF IRREALITIES (SEED VISION)

The seed vision runs like rain or money into the periphery. The lachrymal ducts are like cut blue jewels gazing on the seed vision: keen and escaping. Something ails our colt. Something ails the half-assed thunderbolt or the path the current takes through a flame-colored cord looping through the narrow lot. At the corner of dust and dust, the big girls hunch. Their hair scraped back is a thoroughfare of sight. Their loose bright jerseys. Get those girls inside. The rain shower is a shower of gold is an irruption through the keyhole is: seed money. Enter: cloud of smoke. Enter a hole in the roof that lets the Dove in. A whole that includes the roof, that is, the Seed Vision. The milk arrived sweating in its wax. It wore the stamp of its family of family farms: milk-riddle. It sweats in its skin. It sweats in its rind. It won't give birth in the daytime. It won't give an answer. It won't make a sign. What is it? [an egg] What is it? [a missile] [An envelope] [A capsule] [A shudder at the door] Blood riddle. [One shoulder shoved in.] Day riddle. Rattle and wrack. Adjust the baffle now fumble with the boom mic. Hup! The cow rooted up the vision now lodged between its horns. It can't see it as it pulverizes the market stalls and café tables. It treads the waiter's toe. Back in the kitchen garden, the tuberoses and the fat roots fly in skirts of dirt that flip and subside, momentarily covering the dish-eye of the camera like a rogue's or a child's eye: Under the skirt am I. Now swatted aside. We've finally got the contraption working. We've finally got the picture up. On the barn-eye side of the doublewide, the horn of plenty splits, a showcase staircase. Carpet floods down. It's grey in this take, but in the mind it's split red like a lip. It graces the split-level. It graves. It's gold like a sock in the eye: seed vision. It splits in veins. It lifts in vents. It's a well-made dart or volute: Five hundred dancing girls in lockstep pick their way down the divide to the plucking of strings. Plinth plinth. Here the current splits. Here the joiner, the jack. The coupler. The coaxial and the double-axe. Pick, pick, adze. There's a place for everything in this white-white van that has the pluck of four horsemen though one-fourth the pick-up. It's a floating Nation it's a one-horse town that sleeps with one eye open for the other in the head of the brother under the water or the brother walled out.

Tap tap, that's the hands of the dead, that's a blind man wandered off a page, or that's the rain, rain-delayed in the frame-by-frame, a diamond vision, darling, that'll halve the cost and double the price. Mirror-effect. Lake effect. On the lakeshore, the blue-eyed condominiums are grinning; at their shoulders, their green-eyed sisters sulk. That one has a diamond head. That one wears the plaque of a victim. Look closer: their missing panes. A pendulum blade, a scimitar slices down between the eyes of the sleeper but stops a breath from the bridge of her nose. A hare's breath jerks frantically away on a nonsense path soon hidden in the nonsense of the breakdown, the overgrowth. What city is this. Laced down by empty roads, clever clover knots. The sleeper sprawls in her loose garment, she stirs. The seed hovers, huge as day. It has a clasp, it's halved, dicotylid, it has a valve, it's an engine, it's information flattened and veined inside the case. It's balanced on its slim side, it rolls like a plot device, like something that will explode. A button to engage its mirror, powder to spill and spend. See how it clots and coats: bold. And see how it retracts. It's complex as a mall, as a will. As the dancers withdraw, the set retracts. Like the mayflower: compact. It's closed for the season, to the public. Clicks and flits out. *Pffft.* It's the plan.

TREMULOUS, FIBROUS, CRYSTALLINE, PORTABLE AS THOUGHT

When Flet calls the receptor at seven the next morning, she learns that Secretary Otis has again reported her ill and arranged for a substitute. Flet assures the receptor that she is well, but the receptor tells her that the paperwork has been processed, she's free at least til tomorrow, and rest up.

Is she surprised? Ever since she woke up on the Secretary's couch, Flet has felt herself moving in another dimension, as if she's fallen through the false bottom to another bottom, a lower shelf, the sub-system of the sea. She's walking around looking at the freeform coral, brilliant moving fish and fiery vents. She can't imagine going back to work with this knowledge, the scripts falling into her hands, the words passed back and forth between her and Secretary Otis. Up in the other atmosphere.

What else is under here in the drawer of the sea. The glittering watch. The sea-wreck. The china plates embossed with red and blue writing. The seabed of shattered crockery. Littered with correspondences.

She lifts aside a curtain pane and there on the balcony are the jellied twin boys lifting their thick heads of hair towards each other from the horns of their handlebars. Like dividing moons.

★

Flet arrives at the Ford plant, the huge bleached lot with a few junky cars scattered around and a few gleaming ones, their motors running. The drivers are sealed inside like men in caskets. The cars in the gridded lot make no pattern; this is the type of latitude the Administration encourages. Park where you want! It's a big country. The watchbooth big enough for one man slumps empty and listless as the watchman himself, now out of work, kicking the pavement somewhere, hanging around his apartment complex. As the campaign goes, Security in this Administration is a Brilliant Diamond: Tremulous, Fibrous, Crystalline, Portable as Thought. There is no longer a need for anything so analogue as a man in a booth.

Flet gets out of her car and leans against it, thinking about what to do next. If she makes a call on her flip phone, a record will be read into the log. But, again, who is watching? Who is watching the parking lot now?

Maybe no one.

In response to her call, Mick hunches into the lot with his usual level of discomfort, blinking back the streaming sunlight like an arthropod, an acute whip of the chin over his right and left shoulder prefacing his scuttle to her car. He tells her that, at last, the big cheeses are making final decisions for this weekend's Re-Enactment, that his work is finally done, that word about which plan to put into action should come by midnight at the latest.

"So, what's up, Flet. I haven't seen you for a few days. I heard you were sick. Maybe playing around with your little toys was a bad call after all."

"I wasn't sick."

"Apart from when I'm entrapped by maniacs like you, I never catch anything. Controlled environment equals immune stability? Also: plenty of Sportz Drynk. The yellow kind. So where've you been? Why'd you come in?"

"I've just been cooped up in my apartment. Just waiting, like you, to hear from my boss. I want to go for a drive, I want some company. Want to come along?"

"Uhm, I'm supposed to be in the pod today."

Flet stares blankly at him. Either he'll come or he won't come. But she isn't sure she can trust her own eyes anymore.

Soon Mick is buckled in beside her, the dark belt rumpling his sea-green shirt and biting into his stomach. Flet looks out over her own pale knuckles at the desert colors around her and the glinting asphalt stripe of the road rushing under them. He's homely, it's homey to have him with her. He doesn't ask her where she's headed, since fuel consumption is a requirement of all citizens of Nation, and the aimless drive its unintended corollary. "I live in the other direction," he says now, brightly. "I never drive this way?" Flet smiles as they both relax into the car's hypnotic smoothness.

"Mick, I've been having some trouble with my tracking system. It's shorting out and throwing off my other monitors. Do you know how to disable it?"

Of course he does, leans forward, tap-tapping at the panel. Among the monitors a leaf-green light goes out. He sits back in his chair with a nervous glance at Flet. "We're under the radar," he jokes, then coughs and corrects himself. "Not that it's radar, of course."

"Totally under cover," Flet says evenly, and then she drives them off the map.

★

The road Flet chooses is not barred in any way from the main road, is identified by no signs that would draw attention to it. It is simply not on the map anymore, does not lead anywhere the post-Emergency citizen of Nation would think to go. Flights of tough-looking grass arise on the sere floor as if stitching veins of moisture to the earth. On the shoulder of the road, elephantine grey armatures and rickety brackets arise to hold up signs that have been removed or have fallen into the dust. They twitch in high breezes undetectable from the ground, occasionally shriek. They frame squares of landscape identical with those tessellated from horizon from horizon.

"Flet, I'm trying to be cool with this, but in reality, you're like, blowing my mind. I don't feel right out here. Please pull over," Mick says after some minutes.

She keeps driving, her eyes narrow in the light. The road is pocked sporadically with abandoned convenience stores and gas stations. The half-shadow of a pegasus burnt into a stucco wall, the other half dematerialized into the sky. The severed sun of Pepsi rising or sinking into its neat peel of cloud. These fragmented logos wink at Flet as she drives by them, no sooner glimpsed than appearing in the mirror as their obverse.

"Flet, what the fuck are we doing out here? I told you I left some very important stuff on hold back at the pod."

She says nothing.

"Is this, like, a Psycho thing? Did you rob Secretary Otis, Flet? Are we looking for a Bates Motel? Because I could not do that." A pause. "No, seriously, do you realize you are kidnapping me?"

At this Flet snorts. The corners of her mouth twitch. From the pit of her stomach, a roil of sickness kicks up, but when it reaches her mouth, it's laughter. She sits there laughing like the girl in the commercial. She is "helpless" with laughter and she lifts her hands from the wheel. Mick grabs it, they switch like a horse's tail back and forth on the traffic-less freeway, and then she takes her foot off the gas and they coast to a stop in the middle of the road, nose pointing towards the right shoulder. She looks at him, sighs, pushes the gear to Park and steps out. She does this as matter-of-factly as if arriving at the public library or supermarket, did such places exist anymore.

He gets out too and stares at her over the hood of the car. The color has drained from his face and his jaw is widened in anger.

"The whole crazy-girl thing is not cool anymore, Flet. What are we doing here? Do you want to catch something? Do you want to be killed? Plus, we're not supposed to be here."

"We're halfway to Old Capitol," Flet says.

"No, Flet, no. Do not even think that thought. If you want to mess up your life, why did you bring me with you? I like my life. And my job. I have a very important job. I'm important to people."

"For company."

"You're crazy," he says, almost fondly, but his voice is tighter when he adds, "You shouldn't have done this to me, Flet. I didn't know you were fucked up like this."

Flet looks into the rearview. About fifty feet behind them is a Quickie-Freeze service station, a huge seal balancing an oil can going bland in the sun. "Let's check out the Quickie-Freeze."

"Give me the keys, Flet."

She walks away from him, steps over the ankle-high chain barring entrance to the lot. She can see through the dusty window to a one-room store inside, yellow and red packages of nuts and beef jerky, colas in the dim cases.

"Can you break this glass?" she asks the Mick she sees approaching in the glass behind her.

"Why not," he says, bitterly, picking up a brick lying at their feet like a doorstop. He drives it through the glass, then reaches gingerly through to the locking mechanism. Thin streaks of blood appear on his wrist as he drags his hand back through. He stands outside, turning his head this way and that in the bright light as if having a conversation with himself while Flet enters the dim cinderblock store. On a counter, a wire daisy stand is full of maps and brochures, three tiers of them. She takes the whole thing outside and sits down on the sidewalk in the shade of the store. Mick stands a few steps out into the light.

"I don't feel so good, Flet. I'm bleeding. This dust, it could be anything."

"It's just dust, Mick."

"What's your deal, Flet."

"I just want to go to Old Capitol. I want to see what's there."

"That's totally insane. It's toxic, Flet, it's toxic." He's pleading now.

"Look at all this stuff we could go see. Sights! We could stay in the car. We don't have to touch anything."

"Don't do this to me."

"We've come this far, Mick. I just keep thinking . . . I saw something. I have to go."

"Saw something?"

"In the filetape. About E-Day. It made me wonder."

"You can see anything in filetape. Staged moon landings. Ricky Ricardo. It doesn't mean anything. About real life."

"I'm going either way, Mick. Come with me. Come with me. There are no monitors or cameras out here, they don't even bother. Doesn't that make you wonder? Come with me. I want to know."

THE PRESENT MOMENT AS A DEAD CENTER

Old Capitol has none of the ghostliness, the pittedness that marks the route in, though of course it is deserted. Flet and Mick lace back and forth over traffic control circles, cloverleafs, arabesquing onramps and off-ramps. Signs tell them to merge; they shift lanes and merge with no one, into empty rushing air. Mick is gripping the vinyl door interior with the tips of his fingers, his mouth growing smaller and smaller. He is less and less convinced as they approach Old Capitol, but here they are looping a reservoir full of long-legged birds that rise like machinery into the air as they slowly circle it. They follow the grassy belts of road into the heart of the city, see the cracked reflecting pool filled with brown, stuporous waters, the trees growing irregularly in the formerly groomed arcades. Then the stepped pavilions, founding fathers sitting even more anciently and firmly on their litters. Soon they are facing the wide marble plaza before the Capitol steps going rosy in the light. They drive around and around the Capitol building, retreat and reapproach it, but see no strewn fuselage, no craters, no scorched earth, no evidence, nothing to commemorate what occurred here. No shadows burnt into the ground. Of course workers in white Mylar beekeeping suits or widow's weeds could easily have scraped all that away. Flet isn't sure. She U-turns in the empty boulevard, drives away from the Capitol, wheels the car around again and looks back. They study the building from this distance. Postcard view. They dive back in again and veer right. Rising from a depression to one side, they glimpse the heads and shoulders of oversized marble soldiers picking their way through symbolic wire. They see the statue for nurses and a plinth for army dogs. Red, antique-looking telephones bolted to poles stipple the green malls. Great white buildings bloom everywhere like tombs, though they once had their mundane functions: The Mint and the Postal Bureau. The Investigative Body, the Air and Space Detachment. The Coal and Gas. The Big Game and Wildlife Terrace. The Hearth and Humanity Klatch. The Land Division. The House of Health Statistics. The War Unit. The ark-shaped

Department of Education; Flet lifts one hand off the steering wheel and gives a halfhearted salute. The Department of the Interior. Old Capitol is still intact and representative, like a children's school project, like a game. Replicated on an exact scale of itself: 1:1. Up on the left, Flet sees the limestone Library façade, thinks she can see in its broad flanks the fossils of former life, airholes and squat shells like the hands of tiny ancient babies. As she drives back for the interstate, the flagpole on the Capitol building appears and ducks away in Flet's rearview. It *tsks* and ticks.

★

For all her brazenness, even Flet is reluctant to get out of the car in the basin of Old Capitol. They wheel out of its limits, stop just on the outskirts at a campground, where falling-down picnic tables are still propped in a clearing of orange-barked pine trees right next to the asphalt lot. A dry, tindery smell pervades the place. Flet sits on the ground and leans against one of the unreliable benches. Mick sits belted in the car with the window cracked. Flet leans back and studies the bright hazy fringe of sky through the tops of the pines.

Without shifting his eyes in her direction, Mick says into the windshield: "Do you know how long soil holds on to, like, contaminants? A long time. It's superaccumulative."

Flet leaps instinctively to her feet, grateful to have her rubber soles between herself and the soil.

"You seem happy about that, Mick."

"No, you seem happy about that, Flet. You dragged us out here into the contamination zone like some kind of overgrown canaries."

"Canaries?"

"Like in coalmines. To see what would happen."

"No, I didn't really think about it that way. I just wanted to see what they were closing off out here."

"Well you should have thought about it that way, Flet. See this body? I am not a toned man. Lots of soft tissue here for storing antigens that can come back and bite my ass five, ten, thirty years from now."

"Do you feel sick, Mick?"

"No, I feel angry. Angry at you. Was this worth it? If we die? Did you find what you were looking for, at least?"

"Yes." It's the truth. She expected nothing, and she's found nothing. But what can it confirm, this nothing on nothing. What can a syllogism prove. Or do you have to build a life inside it, this blank and tabular plane.

"That's great, Flet. If you're done subjecting me to random life-threatening experiments for no reason, then please let's get back to the pod."

With a final brush of the dead needles from her clothing, Flet settles herself back into the car. They make the drive back to the Ford plant quickly and in silence.

A POINT OF CONTACT WHICH, ENVISIONED, RECEDES

Tap. A joist falls into joint. Lie down lie down. Lash up and around, run through, secure the tarp. Fit on the water spout. Rise up the ladder. Knit rush to rush. Down into down. Top up, top up. Slow down. Tighten the protecting flank. The living roof. Water collects in a hollow. Runoff colludes. Turbines muddy. The city built in the wake of the pure chute clouds. Sun in a puddle. Mud clots and folds. The foot sinks and the shoe sucks. The show sucks. We have failed to raise the funds. We have failed to appreciate. Do we sink the drain, or do we shuck the footprint. Tup. Lash. Smooth. Stalk.

A raised hand is glimpsed in the water. But this chopper is only equipped with a lens and a spot. Here detail is agony and agony is life. To look is to take part in. To take part of, to get away. Yet always more agony to fructify. A yeasty overpass. A livid parasite. Rumor like a noose, like a root cause and a lie. Butter in the roof. A palmful of powder. A bitter, deciduous pond. By the factory flank. Collects and shines. Outlined in spat ashes, spat gold, the hand. Reads two ways. Bites the hand that reads it. An elevation map. An excavation plot. Sages purging in a toil, eyes mute, because they are too stripped and weary to look the right way, cannot bless the valley or the mutating birds or crabs with soft, useless, multiplying legs.

With the help of the choppers, we're on miracle watch. We balance on the end of a whip, crack wide and ride, hide in the rills and ducts and valleys of air to contemplate the lot. Someone saw a brown eye, though there was no way to tell it. Though there was no way to feel it, someone heard a melting toll. To the face of roiling waters, someone held up a polished plate. Then the water ducked away. Tucked and rolled, and restored its image. Can you see me, visage? Here I am!

LONG, ALONG

Flet wakes up with her mouth chalky. Something unnamable is clear, impels her out of bed and into her workday synthetics. She picks up her briefcase and is out the door. She walks right past her car and out to the shoulder of the low road which is already thick with cars, slow as a vein of honey. No one walks in Nation. It's dangerous to move without the speed, the communications system, the battery, the UV screen of the car. But Flet has less than a mile to go towards the ferry slip; from there she can ride over to the cliffs where the Re-Enactment Day preparations are being made.

Flet picks up signals from the steady colonnade of cars approaching the ferry. Her sight is strange; the sight (of her) is strange. They keep their windows sealed in the haze carved thinner and thinner by exhaust. Two centuries ago, a war begins, the schooner and the flagship haul around in the harbor to turn their flanks on each other. They hold their stings in their flanks. The battle is moral and so will be played out in a set of hazardously thickening components, tonnage of water and cannonade. The leopard and the tawny lion rouse and uncurl in the gut of the scene. They bound up and bat the masts down. They swing the prows around. Men fling missiles, cling to the rigs in rags. The inexhaustible ocean pours in the gunwhales. The guns· slide around. Rats jump away, swimming furiously, and are absorbed into the leopard and the lion. Their energy turns around. For the drinking pulp, the type is being set. For the handbell and hand-crank, for the telegram that will cinch or synch the world tighter. Horns, chutes, and mouths pep up in the obscure town of football geniuses while white wrists raise up a pulpy haze of pom-poms swallowing the knuckled fists within. Local colors shake and swing around. A wave sloshes in the dish of the stadium. The end zone sucks the ball down and the team is absorbed into the floor and the stadium evacuates. First the bat-winged jet, and then the low roll over where the crowd should be like a boulder rolled away from the cave. One lump or two.

It's a drill, our side.

In the filetape, a hand explodes in confetti. The fruit-shaped grenades, the grapeshot explodes. It hits home. Funny continental soldiers run by in blue swallowtail coats and double rows of brass buttons without heads, their blood jumping out of their throats like extinct exclamations. Children hop down the road on the balls of their feet and the whites of their eyes and long, webbed fingers spread out like frogs'. And softhearted Huck ducks a frog back in the water, lowers a wide brim over his freckles and hole-punched, starry eyes and slips on down the blank, affectless river.

Parrots in the home for writers or aged slipper-sailors and sealant sniffers. Salt-corroded. Down to their holey bones. Earrings swing from them like inventory control devices. One guard shot his Irish hunter's ear off, then fastened it on again with a screwlike earring. When it fell off in front of the czar, it was taken for a bad omen like *after me the goose is cooked.* Like *after you, no after you* the thick air-belly crawls through the louvers or prostrates itself, makes like a spoon, lies down in obeisance under the flat tap of the blade. Sword, fern, fan, eyes, hasps of a mustache over which glares the slim-limbed Confederate uncle with one hand to his breast and the features of the landscape dripping away behind him, façades and colonnades picturesquely half-eaten by time, air, distance, going green-grey with asphyxiation, the sky they were only just learning to corrode with gypsum, saltpetre, talc, coal.

It's a drill or a stunt for Re-Enactment Day. The shadow moves slower than the jet over the colonnade of drivers. Flet watches one by one as the drivers' necks crane up like flowers in time-lapse. Though it's their own machine, proudly manufactured just down the road, in the Nation for the Nation, Flet watches each face turn nervous in profile. Then the incomparable roar shoves their necks back down. Progress is slow. The scrub-grass that grows on the shoulder closes around Flet's ankles like a cuff like a shackle like a rattle or pom-pom for the grass-dancing. A helicopter filming the line of cars dips its nose at her like a dragonfly, then turns on her its flank. If it turns its belly or its neck that makes her the alpha male, that makes this line of bulky, fuming cars her rangy pack she'll lead up on the table rocks and look down into the valley. Warming their bellies. Arranging their white hats. Tweaking their fan collars. Their curled wigs of many mansions, many hot-combs in their manservants' packs. The city on the lip of the bay like a decorative flourish on a soup bowl. The wolves extinguished by consensus like pollution long ago ceased to exist, stripped from the roll from the scene of the moment.

Lays of knowledge.

What's shaking: her flip phone. She thinks: Secretary Otis, looking for her. But now she has reached the ferry slip, the blue arched canopy and gold lettering that continually shifts and can't be read. Characters elapse into the air, the spindly poles flex and uproot like standards in a history painting, flying wildly over the scene on its dangerous sharpened point. Like

Curtains, sister.

Seriously.

The stile reads Flet's palm as she boards the ferry. It's been years. She loves its shifting heft. The rest of the passengers stay in their cars. Looking around, she can see filescreens dropping down from the roof, showing realtime footage of the cliff that now shows its tense grey shoulder ahead of them.

Flet lays the closed phone on the flat rail in front of her. She flips it open to a photo of the Secretary's face and a blinking message light. As the deck moves steadily forward, she thinks about removing from the device the tiny weight of her fingertip, sending it flipping into the water to ring with the fossilized fishes in the ringing, bone-cold depths. She wonders if the pollution in the bay is the kind that corrodes or the kind that preserves. Aren't there both? There is no odor out of this bay except for that of the fuel-rainbows gathered like bunting to the sides of the ferry and raying in a train behind. Has the water been totally sterilized, is it vacant, an empty thought, an automatic gesture, like reaching a book from a shelf behind you, this water reaches them over to the land.

THE PRESENT MOMENT AS MOVEMENT INTO

It fell into her hands. It was a talking book, like a flip phone. Like the early days of education media. It lay on the picnic table as her mom was inside mixing mayo and eggs. Her life was in single digits, and her hair was in pigtails. Tea was steeping in a transparent canister. Cancer was sinking into her shoulders to curl up and sleep. Her shirt tied at her shoulders with ribbons. Open the book and read, came a voice from over the fence. It was the voice of the neighbor-child, an adoptee. Flet is the addressee. Her shirt ties on with ribbons. Too much sun; gold goblets are flying through the air, gold couplets, gold cobbler crusts, fried cutlets, gumball lockets, spiders with diadems for eyes. Flet opens the book. It is full of pictures and fine print, but it isn't dirty. Girls are folded up in wings on the top of buildings or step out of the ocean in their bathing suits with one hand on their thighs. One girl stands up out of a giant clamshell, one is embracing a leonine cloud of smoke. One is wearing a blue windbreaker and bikini bottom and she's been swimming in her sneakers and they're grey instead of white. Her hair sticks to her face, and her freckles. Two girls are sisters and in their jeans and T-shirts pose in every room of the house; they also wear Egyptian eyeliner. The rooms are full of texture: silvery tureens and chargers, mirrors, nubbed, oracular aqua-twin bedspreads like star charts in the guest room where the girls sit heavy as rocks. They sit like Scylla and Charybdis. Like Charybdis and Charybdis. They stare at the camera as

Flet's mother comes out of the house and they eat sandwiches together, as

Flet arrives at the cliffs with the rest of the passengers.

The cars immediately re-form their column as they slot off of the boat, angled for the tops of the cliff. Flet sidles off quickly. At the edge of the jetty she removes her shoes and walks a few steps onto the beach which is stiff and sharp like a beach of salt. She looks out over the water but the haze makes it hard to see much. Here on the beach, foil and green glass poke up regularly from the sand in a randomized pattern, a freckly fractal, second jetty stretching into the sand like sea. If the land was sea, if the stars were money, if sunlight dripped in the gutters like rain, if rain were wine, if towers were shuttles, if never the twain. Flet opens her briefcase and fishes out the egg-toy. She tamps it into the sand like it might break open to invent neon rabbit-bird life. But nothing is added to the universe, Flet remembers. Everything stays. She uses the comb to dig out a little crevice in which she then buries it.

Flet follows the beach around to where it will eventually meet the cliff-face. It is a longer stretch than it has looked from the road or the ferry, and the texture of her bare feet pushing into the sand sends a prickly shiver up to her scalp. She begins to wonder: what is to be done? by which she means: what am I doing here? She leans against the rockface, into the foot of shade that is available at this hour. Looking back, she sees cars steering up the white concrete ramp from the jetty. The air directly over them shimmers and shakes like a god in hiding. Her head hurts: dehydration, but what can she do? She doesn't want to think. She wants to watch something.

She pulls out her flip phone and watches Secretary Otis in beige jeans, a purple shirt, and a lavender neckerchief, boots, a wide hat. She is on safari in the parking lots at the Cliff, high above Flet's head. She grins and waves at the families in the cars; Flet knows there is a device for jamming the filescreens as she approaches, and that's why the passengers in the cars snap their heads so fiercely for the windows. The children, in particular, clamor for Secretary Otis, having seen her on so many of their programs. When she has passed, they turn back to the notebook-sized filescreens and wait blankly for them to turn back on.

Flet flips her phone down and continues her march, keeping in the shade, though she knows it will make the journey longer. She has taken only a few steps when her phone rings again. Secretary Otis.

"Flet. How are you feeling."

"I can meet you tomorrow for the Re-Enactment," Flet answers.

"I think it best if you take your time recovering. I can arrange it. Call it a leave."

"Recovering from what?"

"You seem upset, exhausted. Perhaps the job is too much for you."

"You're firing me?"

"A leave, Flet. We'll talk in a few weeks. Call it a month."

The silence is heavy, packed with exchange. "What about what we saw." "What about it, Flet." "I believe in it. I'm starting to believe it." "Well then, you really are sick." "I think you believe it too." "I'm sorry, you're mistaken." "I know you, Lonnie. We manufacture filetape all the time; the Administration could have manufactured the E-day filetape." "By the same logic, someone could have manufactured this conversation, too." "Someone did." Pause. "Leave it, Flet. We're leaving it here."

The silence flattens by a degree as Secretary Otis hangs up. Flet continues walking, but veers slightly, until she is not in the shade but in the sun. She stumbles on. She can't have far to go. But her head feels heavy, her body paradoxically light as if she might fume up and blow away through the top of her own head. She trudges a few steps farther, and sees that the cliff is starting to turn. She pauses to study its elephantine, mottled flank. She realizes she is hallucinating as a door in the rockface opens and a Martyr-Leader emerges with his staff, walking down the air as if on steps. Then another, then another. She starts to swoon as the first cluster reaches beach-level, shakes hands, and goes their separate ways. Just then she is caught up in strong arms.

ON AN ADJACENT PLATFORM

She wakes up on a plain of tents spreading out before her, hundreds, perhaps, variegated in hue but of the same iconic plan, none larger than would fit two adults lying side by side. Their schematic neatness makes her think of simple instruments: banjos, fiddles, clarinets, the human body folded at its joints. These tents resting here by common agreement could clamber up on their poles and gallop in a herd into sheer, wispy, decorative cloud-sky. Flet turns around to inspect the low tent from which she has come. Born again. From a hole in the ground. The outside is weighed down in a hopalong pattern of round flat stones and jars holding brown liquids of varying transparency, grains, meat twisted and dried like expressive hands, and plenty of buttons and poker chips, chess pieces, checkers, other plastic flotsam. A garland of aluminum—safety pins, pop-tabs, forks bent around their tines—hangs around the outside of the tent. Ducking her head and shoulders back in, she can see the inside stacked with antique media disks and magazines in heaps and piles. She also sees her briefcase and gratefully snatches it from the tent.

People are starting to seep in at the left edge of the encampment and move purposefully through its mazy lanes as if they know its grid from above. Flet moves against the flow. They stare at her in her stained office clothes, pass her, and stare at her back. Remembering some instinct from the time of populous cities, Flet fixes a hard, even angry look on her face and keeps moving. The ground is soft, slightly wet beneath her feet. She looks down in surprise. Her bare feet are cut, burnt and swollen, unfamiliar to her as an animal's.

She sinks down in front of the nearest tent. A woman emerges from the tent and kneels down to meet her face. Foolish, the woman says.

Flet studies the woman, squarely built but strong-looking in her purple T-shirt, her heavy grey hair pulled back. Her face is thickened with sun. Her eyes are ink-black. Flet says, Are you here for the Re-Enactment?

Don't you know how to travel? Sturdy and light, the woman responds, yanking Flet up by her elbow and into the tent. She barks at Flet to take off her white blouse and pulls a folded black T-shirt out of a neatly tied plastic bag. The shirt swims around Flet's body and feels cool. She looks down and reads its upsidedown letters: Humane Society of Georgia. Don't know what we can do about shoes for you. I've got shoes, Flet suddenly remembers, reaching inside her briefcase for her slender pumps. The woman looks at these and laughs. I'd advise you toss those out.

Are you here for the Re-Enactment? Flet tries again.

We're all part of it, right? We're all part of it, or it's not a Re-Enactment.

After a pause, the woman continues: How'd you get lost from your people?

I'm not here, Flet says, and then she falls back into cold sleep.

★

When Flet emerges from sleep again the tent is empty. She steps out to see a grid of fires burning across the camp, making its location and size visible and quantifiable to the Administration helicopters she'd seen surveying the traffic that morning. There's something about these people's resourcefulness, their apparent identification with one another, which sits strangely with Flet, and which she's certain falls outside what the Administration had in mind for the participation of its citizenry. She scans the sky systematically, rung by rung, for a pack of stars that could shift into a helicopter's runners, for the path cut by a loping, lazy set of lights. She knows the names of a handful of constellations, and now phrases from remote conversations slide into the gaps of her knowledge as she gazes on the configurations: The Balance of Powers. The Buried Head. The Flight of the Martyrs. The Flight of Steps.

The Donation. The Detonation. The Retrieval. The Arrival. But there is no shape in the sky called The Re-Enactment.

And now it comes into Flet's mind to wonder whether this gathering is an entirely unique event, or has been going on regularly for years—since the Emergency, prior to it. Considering the flatness of the plane from a point far out in the sky, she gropes for a further possibility: that this instant has been going on, simultaneous to the rest of the universe, for some time. For all time.

A REELING

Now she was reeling. There were probably three. Three flips, three falls. Close to a ceiling stippled with holes—for breathing. Once on a rail stretched between sunlight and tall fragrant bushes that dripped with a water of wasps. And once wrapped in blankets from house to rocking boat. The yard was gone. It was night and freezing lightless except for a shattering eye that swung from its stalk on the boat to glare at the heaving yard. Possibly the yard always dissolved at night, went black and insolid, grew a rushing murky hide that clambered from the inlet and shoved with its shoulder at the shrieking clapboard flank of the house. No legs and no mouth, no eyes. Once hurried into a blue vinyl car and driven over a field of melting tar, her hurt wrist visibly breathing like a pet in her lap. Once under a cold bank of light. The stars and the coins looked so pure and pretty but ran dirty down to earth. She learned this when she leaned close to taste the runoff in the door-lock. A hand slapped her hard on the neck, her teeth ground the lock through her lip. It graveled her knees and bit starred marks in her palms.

How had she climbed to the platform of such improbable height? An oversight, wedged in a crawlspace between the top plinth and the ceiling. This time she leapt. On the splintering rail leaning backwards into a wall so solid with scent she could almost rest against it. This time she fell. To the floor of the shuddering boat. This time as she landed the batteries shook in their shunts, the static barked and commanded, the compass needles spun around, and a huge wave converted from roiling earth to ripping sky and howled and flexed with white light.

Each fall made a channel. Each time split. Each catastrophe acquiesced to its event, welcomed her into its principles. What lapse had allowed them to conduct her hence. Calm at the center like all storms and narrow enough for one traveler. Through primary-hued sweating structures, faces and arms of little children poking from slides and bars. Her spread hands ripped with thorns and closed on water, a stinging fragrance stopped her mouth and her pasted-over eyes, and when she opened her mouth to scream she was converted to a metallic fish that could breathe through a laking mask.

The blanket bound her as she fell against knees and landed in a pit, face up; through her matted hair she saw a rocketing display of light that shot up from one side, rocketed and then whined high-pitched and metallic for some minutes as the grownups hunched and cried out, sound balled up and the crowded boat whipped from side to side. She could not get free of the blanket and began to panic and scream until two hands grabbed her by the elbows and hoisted her high. She kicked the blanket away. The cold air whipped against her burning skin and her mother grabbed her and wrapped her up again, the boat stabilized and began to move towards the terrible sound, towards town and the ripped-open plant feeding nothing but hurling its energy into the sky. It was either that or out to sea, and the instruments were shot, their blips and needles queerly jolting towards the little girl wrapped in the quilt. An odor of blood and lilacs filled her mouth and nostrils. Rough carpet and sweet rainwater rubbed at her drained yellow face.

★

Flet wakes to the tent blown away if she were never sleeping in the tent. She sits up in a dry slick bed. Checks and receipts: bank waste. Her face caked, she knocks the chalk from the seams of her eyes. Her lids and cheeks are cushy, swollen. Inflamed. She rakes up a breath cut with the powder that fills her veins. Decay. Dust from a sap. Lowered visor. Grand elapse.

She makes a fist; it aches where her muscles contract, like a ghost hand gripping her upper arm. She spreads her fingers: a coin in her palm. Solid money. It catches the sun. She hasn't touched money since her childhood, since there's no more circulation. She can pick out the grave face that winks in relief.

She stands up. The landscape: sand, chalk, talc, particulate, crumbling as she tries to pick it out. Reason, identify: a low yellow cinderblock wall. A flaking single chain stretched across two flaking posts at the parking lot. Easy enough to walk around to the fleet of hot cars. The asphalt lane flecked with cans and foils. A light that dances like a sediment of day across these surfaces. A slow, bottom-of-the-sea progress in the tide of light. Exhausted garments that want to hang behind her. Her hair in odd gritty coils, one hank stuck to her shoulder and one curled high on her neck. She bends her neck down to look in a wing mirror; a greasy, dry whiteness like a sickly mask. It's no closer than it appears, she's willing to bet. Cast as the lately dead, her head breaks through to a layer of lightness, her weight lessens.

Next: an inkling of static, grey, a sound the hue of cigarette ash. Down below ankle level, maybe down a slope or cliff to the left. She doesn't want to lift even a foot toward the sound, but her mind swoops down to circle it: attention, dumb as a toy. Makes a thin ring like a line in blue pen or a razor at the pulse point: inkling. And then a sudden amplification, a snarling, the shoulders of the biplane tear and hurl themselves into vision. Flet drops down between two shining cars as the plane leaps up, circles, slices, incises the air with white exhaust. Some switch thrown, its engines silence and it glides off, inland, out of sight. Next, a sound of fabric tearing and the two blue fighter jets knife into view, slow and close enough to turn to Flet the plates in their bellies before they, too, convert to silence and shrink off.

For a moment, this silence holds: full, even, yet dynamic, the surf behind and below her, the cry of the flourishing garbage birds, her fat heart thumping like a hungry child. It amazes Flet how violently, how tight a confinement the crown of her head has become. Then, it splits: a thin streamer of yellowish static breaks from a speaker propped high above Flet's head, and is blotted out by a tremendous black burst that presses her neck down like a boulder; she's fetal with supporting the weight of such a globe. The sound is a rock womb trying to break apart. Then, from under it, a thin hissing sound of rockets, a scorching white chemical stench that backflips as the wind reverses and goes gusting down to fill the bowl-shaped amphitheater where Flet now realizes the Re-Enactment is taking place.

A MACHINE AMID MACHINES

It is a landscape of still motors. Flet's head in her arms, her nose pressed up against her knees, she smells chalk instead of her own skin. She smells an engraving: damp paper: a body or its picture crumbling. The hulks of cars all around her like a city of the dead. Hurl their shadows straight down. She hopes the grit on her skin will stop her from burning up entirely; that is no way to go. She hears motors like wood bees or dragonflies, heavy, low to the ground, active somewhere far below her. She hears smaller insects high up in the sky, tinny and headless. Or like the humming of ancient fluorescent lights tacked high up in the sky. The low, cycling engines move closer, up the cliff road, toward the mouth of the parking lot, and she knows that, though the cliff below her offers crevices in which to hide, it will be impossible to reach them without detection. And how long will she hide? And from what or whom? And now she feels the asphalt hum with a heaviness, the asphalt and the tires like two bodies greeting, a pliant, square tissue of noise that shades out in every direction. The machine enters the far side of the lot and makes slow, steady progress up the first lane. But it pauses for nothing. There is nothing to stop it as it passes windshield after windshield, hood and grille overheating in the noon sun. Flet listens to the sound widen and climb in pitch, spread out, keep moving. It's an amazingly fibrous sound, dense and intricate, the many pinions and belts and sparks and bearings that flap and pound in the veins. It seems to Flet's concentrating mind a passionate sound.

Now is her chance. While the machine makes its next turn, she can double over backwards, scramble for the cliff edge, drop down below the line of sight of the vehicle before it can resume its searching. Maybe land on a root or a shrub, maybe dash her head, maybe tumble straight down into the sterile, inorganic ocean. But she doesn't move. She is through moving.

She wants the machine to find her.

And now it moves closer from her left, the deep red cloak of its sound reaching her, dropping over her; as it moves closer she is held closer and closer to its center.

And now it stops directly in front of her, blocking the channel of sky at the end of these two cars. But its noise does not stop. Flet raises her head slightly, the bridge of her nose against her forearm. A second sheath of diesel odor gathers around her. She lifts her chin against her forearm, shakes her hair away. In the van before her, a white-wrapped figure in a treated visor turns the black eye of a camera in her direction. She stares at this vision through the eaten air. When she has it memorized, she turns her head to the right, lowers her cheek against her bony, dusty arm, and closes her eyes.

She is lifted and opens her eyes as she is thrown into the back of the van. The white-clad figure fastens his camera to an armature that extends from the van's ceiling. He yanks at her shoes, then takes a pair of shears from his belt and cuts them off at the laces. He tears her skirt down and cuts the shirt from her torso. At the sight of her human body she thinks he pauses a split second, but this second is indistinguishable from the sequence of before and after, the sequence that keeps him in motion. He reaches around her to the nozzle of a tank lashed to the van's interior. He fits a transparent hose to it and turns a stream on Flet that feels like water. With a jerk at her shoulder, he flips her around, douses her hair, and a white, sticky clay begins to run down her body. He chases this away with the current, then turns the hose on the grate that opens in the floor, driving down the runoff. Flet realizes this liquid isn't just water but has a slightly bitter taste. He turns its considerable pressure on her shoulders, her back, her legs, her buttocks, reaches for her nails, the bottoms of her feet, her cheeks, her neck. He sprays down the interior of the van. He lets her stand there as it drips away. He opens a sealed package and pulls out a towel treated with a powder, and roughly dries her. Then he lifts out a garment like a hospital gown; strings flap down the side. She ties these with sore fingers. She feels as if a layer of skin has been rubbed away. He grabs her by the waist, lifts her out of the van, carries her to the cab, and slams the door after her. He circles around to the back, drives the instruments back in to their places, and slams the back doors shut. Then he returns to the front of the van, clambers in, pulls a hard plastic divider from the seat to the dashboard, separating himself from Flet. She leans against the locked door as the whole compartmentalized universe lurches forward. Through the boxy rumbling, she hears a flock of blades above them.

FLET 2

GEOGRAPHER'S LOG

We had not planned for the girl, so we did not have a safe-room ready outside the compound where we could limit her contact with auxiliaries. At any rate, the driver had brought her in, and once he had brought her in, who would issue the order to bring her out again? As geographers without a working map of our new surroundings, as aging men wary of traveling beyond known quadrants, as sequestered men locked down without word from our superiors, we were in every sense directionless. In response to a remote interior welling as piquant and keen as a silvery spring, I volunteered to search out suitable quarters for her. I felt a headiness that was almost undergraduate, moving gridless through unmarked corridors, but soon discovered a chamber in the main complex that seemed ideal for our prerogatives; it featured a nurse's bed and a heavy blanket, a cabinet of long expired gauzes and tinctures, and a nauseating painting of mallards in a gruel-gray sky that encouraged anyone gazing upon it to turn his or her thoughts to matters beyond this world. It was not even necessary to sedate her, had it been possible for us to elect that course. She slept through the first forty-eight hours without breaking the surface. Without seeming to come up for air. She became a conspicuous absence from our deliberations, though to my own mind she was ever present, like a priceless icon tossed from a fleeing vessel, turning slowly and clad in a mantle of bubbles as it descends through the depths.

Those first news-less, noiseless days seemed like an eternity; time went almost internal in its measureless, expanded pace. We felt invulnerable in what we came to know as a disused animal-feed plant, checkered with rusting acres and exfoliating silos and docks, but also sightless and invisible, unable to absorb or release information into the rest of the world, a world that dawn's angles told us was still there, outside the sightlines of our perimeter cameras.

We had been leaving messages for days at all the old numbers in the voicemail system, and we must have hit a live box because one morning a safe scientist arrived at the compound to evaluate the girl's state. He arrived in a protective suit, though we had in shifts been sitting with and silently studying the girl in no more than our shirtsleeves, lit only by the corridor light and inoculated only by curiosity and the amber tumblers in our hands. We kept away while he drew blood and measured the gases dissolved therein, checked her pulse and pupils for impairment, clipped hair and cut fingernails, punched a sample of skin. He concluded that she was basically unharmed, since the gases had blown away from her, across the amphitheater and out to sea to break up over the channel, according to preliminary conclusions. She was suffering dehydration and malnourishment and he would call for an auxiliary, after all, to oversee an IV, if none of us were equipped. None of us were equipped. He eyed us through the plastic visor of his hood, each blue snake in the caduceus stamped on his breast also glaring through keen, jewel-cut eyes. Having refastened all his snaps and seals, he departed, carrying away from us the first vials of our girl.

His auxiliary arrived also clad in white Tyvek, his fingers nervously gripping and regripping the black handle of his titanium case. But it took only the boredom of a few short days before he removed his gloves, flexing his hands in the filtered, locked-down air, and then, since the seal had been compromised, his jacket, and then finally his hood. I found him sitting in just a T-shirt, trousers, and thick white boots, filling out his carboniferous log book or flipping the grimy pages of a tabloid retrieved from some corner of the plant, his robust neck brushed now and then by the tendrils of a listing artificial palm, thickly sprouting from artificial sphagnum in a wicker basket set at spies' distance from the laminate walnut desk.

"Slow in here?" I asked him, settling myself on an orange vinyl visitor's chair.

"Hmm," he responded, turning a page, though his response may also have been no more than the drawing of a particularly thoughtful breath.

"And our patient?"

"Same."

"Should we be worried?"

"No. We're feeding her, I got solids here for her when she's ready, she's breathing on her own."

"Is she in . . . is this some type of coma?"

"No. She wakes up on her own about twice a day, I help her into that little toilet, then it's back to sleepy-time for her."

"She's drugged?"

"Well, I give her the mixture they told me to give."

"How long have you been reading that same magazine?"

The auxiliary grins. "Weeks. It's interesting, though. All this stuff happened so long ago and I never heard about it. Mermaids making babies with fat old alien men. By now there's probably like a secret race of mutants growing up underwater and just waiting to take over from human beings."

"Maybe she's one of them," I joked.

"Her? Naw. They've got loads of filetape of this girl. They know exactly who she is."

"Oh?"

"Yeah," he said, turning back to his newsprint.

"You're in touch with the main building?"

"I call in."

"When do you hear that the filetape feed will be restored?"

"They're working on it," he said, "but soon, I hope. They've got it unjammed residentially, I hear, but not at the government stations, go figure. Part of the plot, I guess. At first I was happy not to have any more bad news. I was, like, a little bit relieved. But now I could use some distraction. You know, watching some sick girl sleep all day."

I cleared my throat. "I'd be happy to spell you. There's really nothing for us to do, either. At first we formulated a set of protocols. They're all ready when we get the call. But now, we're just waiting. Like everyone else."

"Spell me, huh?"

"Yes. Like in shifts?"

The auxiliary took a long breath. "Naw. That's not what I'm supposed to do."

★

Despite herself, I think, the girl got stronger, and I could detect at my afternoon visits, the same time every day, a change in her prone body, an alertness in her shoulders and back, turned to the auxiliary and me. She was awake. As she recovered, she also seemed to grow younger, an illusion created by her sleep-rumpled hair, her mottled but flushing cheek, and her spindly, weakened limbs. By then the filetape had been restored even to our offices and we were again getting messages from the world, messages that told us not to act but to continue in our state of readiness, the readiness that made us Still the Nation, Still. Still, it cheered us. We met daily to evaluate our protocols in response to the news briefings, wrote up optimistic and defiant releases in case this was the day our lowly bureau was to be brought officially online again. By late morning, what makework we could develop was done and we were free to stroll the grounds, vigilantly of course, watch filetape, or visit our patient.

It was my idea to move the filetape screen from my own office into the sickroom itself, ostensibly for the distraction of both parties, but also for my own pleasure. I liked to sit with them in the dark, myself in the visitor's chair, the orderly with his feet on the desk, the girl leaned up against the wall, the three of us sipping cola or rehydrated fruit-juice in silence while horse hooves beat the desert to smoke, heroes concealed their faces in Mexican shawls, and bullets careened through chrome-colored ether before our three sets of wakeful and watchful eyes. It was as if we were memorizing needful information we had known all our lives.

Then one afternoon I arrived to find the auxiliary packing his materials back into his case. The young girl was nowhere to be seen. At dawn that day, a transport had arrived for her; he would be reassigned. He began layering on the laborious segments of his suit, and before he could fasten on his last glove, I shook his hand. He shook it carefully, and confessed he was not sorry to go.

Then the room was empty again, except for the mallards still struggling to get free of their thick acrylic layer, the spent tabloid, and the filescreen, that day with its lunging and pontooning GI's scrambling across exploding beachheads like baby turtles bloated and reversed.

EXEMPLARY DAYS

It is time to become exemplary again. This is the lesson. A female auxiliary with carrot-colored hair, fake-looking white skin and cerulean foil makeup spread wide as a gingko leaf over each eye is stationed in the white chamber. The girl is a greener white. There is something wrong with her diet, perhaps. She does look drained. Yet everyone is pleased with her attitude. She eats. She watches the filetape. She gets up for a walk down the hall. She wears a hospital gown though she is not sick with anything detectable. Sat at the long table and instructed, she follows. She can sign her name. She can manipulate the filescreen controls. She can use wires to connect each drawing of a barnyard beast with its name and the sound it makes. The map lights up. A crowing fills the room.

She does not choose to use her own voice. This is the verdict of the resident. She can, but does not choose to, use it. This is the last word. But not a problem yet. The improvised process goes smoothly. She is tested, she is filmed, she is bathed, and then she is left to sleep through the days and watch filetape.

Finally it is decided that her physical recovery is complete; she must now regain her stamina and her voice. But how to do it. The auxiliary arrives with a bag of brightly colored clothing, trousers and blouses and a jacket each in a separate color bright as a prayer flag, and a pair of red shoes. Dressed this way, like a very small child, the girl is meant to come into her youth again. Her healthful youth. The auxiliary leads her out of the chamber and down the gleaming corridor, up a green tiled staircase and onto the roof.

It takes some moments to adjust to the shock of light, flung, coursing off every sightline, that greets the two women at this height. At their feet is grey-white asphalt; a cement wall runs waist-high along the edge, beyond which a superheated plane of air shimmers before the flanks of white-tiled towers rising up on all four sides. All that can be seen looking upwards is a brilliant shaft leading to a whipped blue oblong sky floating many stories above them, making a channel so vertiginous one could fall up into it almost as easily as down. Asphalt giving strangely beneath their feet, the two walk dutifully around the perimeter four, five times, and then stop. The auxiliary with her metallic circled eyes worries at her watch, then the skin beneath her watch. How long to prolong this exercise? What in this mineral outlook is there for the girl to see?

When they go inside again the corridors are the green of undeveloped film, then filled with crimson and magenta plaques and plates that flow from the periphery to nowhere as the women shift their heads. A corpuscular tide. The auxiliary deposits the girl on her cot, with a glass of water, then elapses into the corridor to make her annoyances known to someone on the end of her fly-black plastic flip phone.

INSIDE THE SKULL, INSIDE THE CELL

Augur or referee? On the face of the soundproofed ceiling, a colony of acne pits. On the inner walls of the beehive tomb, a colloquy of painted men. Wrestling, mating, struggling, bent over their, ha-ha, staffs. The pinholes rejoice and swarm. What are they walling in and wailing out. That staff he holds is for the divination of the sheaf of birds roping off the sky—no, this view is no longer held. That staff he holds is for the divination of points in the wrestling match. Q: What augury's like an auger in the eye. A: A "piercing" vision. Quack, the ceiling's underside. The girl stands on the cot and rests her fingers. A queer dimension where fingers flutter space open and the eyes study shades. Inside this beehive glade. Turf wound. Cool place to think for seasons. Maundering thought: How to force speech again through this cerement brain. It's limp and leathery as Miss Emily on the long absconded chaise. "The figure with the slingshot seems like he will actually hit a bird." "The figure leaning over the boat emits a genuine concentration with his task of catching a fish." "One can imagine that these boys dived and climbed up again many times a day during the summers of their youth." Many youths these boys dived and climbed, many summers again one can imagine. *Tap tap* with your stick, a toothy, tony euphony. Meanwhile time splays in every direction like flowers in a vase. Meanwhile many augers dive. No white-gloved lady traffic-saint can force it to align.

On the groomed, precocious grounds, the staff circles, the staff raises arms, pins sheets, the staff raises funds for a vacation date, the staff raffles, in white cotton garments, scrambles and forays, the staff bundles away. The French boy sticks his thumb into a plum and invents an alphabet in relief. The staff punches messages and places them in the jar. The jar fills with the number of numbers guessed. How many staffers makes one hundred percent. A snake in the grass hints: dot dot dot. Meanwhile the birds with their flock-brains hang an augury in the sky. They hang on airily. They pierce it with an awl, scrawl letters in fluid. The fluid humor drones and drains away. The birds abscond to their nests to nurse their wounds, wound with shawl fronds, blonde locks, magnetic wires, identification photos, food stamps, fingerprints, shreds of electric tape. Who wields the listening beam that can read this plate.

Beneath the punch-bowl sky the staff lays the examining table. The light pearl grays. An auxiliary tilts the spot. When will the consultant surgeon arrive? Meanwhile, above the lights-out girl the staff is saying grace. Take this body into the body of time.

GEOGRAPHER'S LOG

One afternoon in particular I like to revisit, as I stand on these heights, running my hands over the stippled, flat-faced bulbs set into the parapet, which have long since burned out. I've opened closet after closet looking for replacements, peered into mouldering cardboard boxes of silverfish and file folders, cheap pens, stamp-pads, a shelfful of souvenir paperweights etched with an eagle with crossed cornstalks in its talons, pushpins, whiskey, golf balls, even, in a cement basement chamber so crammed with heavy file cabinets as to mock up a mini-labyrinth, a half-empty carton of hypodermics, tucked in shadow at the very top of one slate-grey tower of drawers.

But no lightbulbs suitable for illuminating the rooftop terrace.

It is the understood practice of myself and my colleagues to go to our separate corners of the compound once the morning's meetings are concluded. I suppose in this way we pantomime the industriousness that once did occupy us; we are saving face, if only for each other, by avoiding each other's faces. It was on such an afternoon I stood, taking not so much the air as the heat, when I felt a pain leap up my right arm, then course back down to my throbbing hand. At first I thought I was having a heart attack, but then remembered it was the left arm that is supposed to ache and go numb in those circumstances. I looked down and saw that the flesh on the back of my hand was reddening; a few moments later it had swollen around its sorest point, and then I realized that I had actually been stung by some type of insect that had made its nest amid the disused lamps.

Is it strange to report that a sort of euphoria spread through me, some adrenal miswiring, I suppose, and as I withdrew into the cool of the staircase and plunged without seeing through the darkened halls I was returned to the footpaths and channels of boyhood, the summer place in Vermont, wet grass and toothed brambles, back when time was not one long flat desert noon. We had use of the seasons then, or they had use of us, turning us into new pastures and to their purposes, one of which was marked by the red and black raspberry bushes that formed a border between the ironed lawns of our great aunt's house and the rotting apple sweetness of the farm. On first arrival at the house, or at the earliest point escape could be made from the building's oblong parlors, we would rush out to revisit landmarks we remembered from the previous summer, the trees whose branches formed natural footholds, a twisted and cobra-like root nursing a well of mud, and particularly the thicket of berries, which were always sour on our arrival, small and tight. Hurling ourselves past these berries at least six times daily, we would somehow always miss the point of ideal firmness, but finally reach for the fruit at the exact moment it would give way and drop into our hands from touch alone, without the force of plucking, smearing our fingertips with juice and scratching our forearms and hands as we leaned into the thorny tangled canes. Then at least one of us would dislodge a bee or a wasp with his harvest, and this same stinging wailing sweetness would fill first his arm and then his lungs as it filled mine now as I ran—did I run?—through the corridors to the chamber where we kept the girl.

"A bee sting, would you believe it?" I said into the darkened room, where a flickering filetape showed torch-bearing divers plumbing a reef's brilliantly occupied and improbable crenellations. Both the girl and the auxiliary looked at me, she with her mouth open, he with his firmly shut. "Or a wasp, I didn't see it." The auxiliary rolled his eyes, snapped on a desk-light, and opened his case to see what incidental salves might be tucked inside it. In the end he prised out the stinger and I settled for some artificial ice to cool the spot. But as I looked over my upraised, towel-wrapped arm at the girl, how the glare from the picture-glass lit the crown of her head, I could see her smiling to herself, or at me, or most immediately at the image she faced, neoprened divers sinking deeper and deeper into their pursuits.

That evening I revisited a precinct of the compound to which I had not recently strayed, a sort of subterranean lounge, although it was aboveground, with elaborately brocaded walls and an aquamarine carpet that, lit only by emergency lights from the hall, seemed to rise around my feet. This was some type of executive meeting place, I surmised, done up to look like a civilian nightspot, complete with knobby green candle globes on the tables and hemicircular leather booths. At the center of the room, disturbing sightlines, was an aquarium elaborately lit from above, emptied now except for a collection of hatbox and pillbox and compact corals that, dried to the faintest pink-and-white, made the tank look like the surface of a woman's vanity. Nothing was changing in this model of lifelessness; in this case the ghost audience had well exceeded its· ghostly exemplar by disappearing altogether. I went behind the bar and felt in its deepest recess where a few cool, heavy bottles remained intact. I carried one like a dim torch through the halls as I made sharp turns for my sleeping quarters, meaning to deposit it with the auxiliary at our next meeting, by way of thanks.

AUXILIARY VIEW

At last no further instructions arrive. The end of the improvised protocol is reached. The girl has advanced as far as she is going to advance within the limited, understimulating confines of the compound. This is at any rate the opinion of the auxiliaries, who have themselves advanced to the very limit of their boredom and glower at its edges like a phalanx of bored mercenaries. The girl herself seems, at times, bored, a promising sign. Thick manuals are laid on the table in her chamber, and she has been recorded as perusing them: guides to the post-Emergency structure of the government, education and evacuation procedures, maps and plans, fuel consumption codes, most dampish and aged and made anyhow obsolete by the most recent set of catastrophes. Whether these manuals are meant to occupy her or heighten her boredom and thus encourage her to feel the contours of her own returning will and mind has not been specified.

Finally a day arrives when the main auxiliary, her wide-painted eyes like the blown-out orbits of some nocturnal mammal, enters with a crate of new clothing, a briefcase, a clipboard, a pair of dark-framed glasses, a hair-clip. As she takes each item out of the box, she holds it up and shows it to the girl like a magician preparing to perform a trick. She then leaves the room for ten minutes. When she returns to the room, there is Flet, the girl in the filetape, business-suited though somewhat haphazardly groomed, peering into the empty box like the last audience member to leave the theater trying to glean from abandoned props and mirrors the secret of the disappearing act.

INSIDE THE SKULL, INSIDE THE CELL

What it's like is a schoolhouse-red–painted wooden cottage set at the bottom of a steep slope. The macadam road with its yellow dashed line so thick and clear as to appear drawn on with crayon runs at the top of the slope. The hill descends more gently behind the cottage, spreads into a laking valley of treetops, roofs, a needley steeple and parking lot where a basketball is pushed against gravity and re-ups through a clanking hoop of chains, falling in synchrony and euphony with a soft platoon of thin sneakers. But between the road and the house is a steep, violent reach, so steep that it looks bitten from the earth by huge jaws, or shorn with a giant knife. A carpet of fiery leaves fully covers this lawn like tears and scales and even teeth, as if an incinerating dragon had wept and dematerialized as it flew from its burning lair out of the side of the hill and into the ether. It was onto the back of this dragon or some invisible airy flank that Flet expected to tumble as she took her first step down from the hill's narrow crown, the friend who lived there also beginning the climb down in her periphery as rubbery exhaust from the departing school bus hung in Flet's nose and mouth. It was terrifying to see the ground dropping away below her buckled school-shoe as she tried to slant her sole to the angle of the leaf-slick slope. Below her, now, her friend was like a doll dropped in water, her mussed braids lifting as she fell away. Flet tried to concentrate by looking straight ahead—that was how not to be afraid of heights, she been told, though it was not heights Flet exactly feared now but depths, a smashing plunge. Looking straight ahead, she cast her eyes on the hovering gutter and the roof, and the sensation that she could in the next moment step onto the roof made her feel as if she'd swallowed her Easter gloves, a pair of clothy twisting hands at the center of her gut. So she closed her eyes and took step after step. With each step she drilled down a cold granite channel, a stone staircase she descended with her right foot always first, her right shoulder turned into the rock. When she slipped at last, she was relieved to breathe as she sank through cold and acidic pools and channels, and when she hit the red side of the house, she burst and expanded, was atomized and passed through its walls, dispersed at once to penetrate the corners, to become a portion of the ceilings and curtains, the manmade tiles and the rough fibrous carpetscape, the fiberglass tubs and tickling insulation, the bone-cold pipes, the plastic sheaths and cords and shelving, the motors and the drains, the sockets and conducive plugs, the buried copper wiring as keen as her gnawing incisors and, in the dark, her glimmering eyes.

★

What miniature friend is this? Its teeth a set of thirty-four, each point glittering on the printout, its orbital swollen, its eye that lolls. It is without its reflectors, without beam, without visor, but goes out bare-skulled into the brutal toxic current on long misevolutionary feet. It ruts, rolls, and scurries in the infrared feed. Red dust rolls up to hold it. Its image leaps from itself to the rover, from the rover to the satellite, from the satellite to our observers, pocket-protected and rowed in their rows like sagging teeth. They leap up when they behold, perhaps a mite that traveled on the lens, perhaps an authentic alien being gambling for market share, gamboling for all it's worth, desperate to attract our conquistadors to its algebraic lair of dry riverbeds and bazaars. Bric-a-brac. Brackish feed. Perhaps a dream or a group delusion; we raise our bald pates in wonder and alarm, as if we could drink from them, and drink them to the lees.

A coffee break: We all glaze and daze to our hearts and circuitry. We refocus the instruments by waving a six of hearts before the screen. And now in an evolutionary reversal, our subject enters the abyssal zone, coasts a leathery purse, a mermaid's pittance dropped into the depths. The camera with a tracking light tracks it sauntering asunder. An elaborate knotwork card that flips and flashes its magnetic markings, a hologram of a flapping bird, incised with viral information, it lodges in the sand. Turning its head or its tail in molecular arraignment, the silver skate/ that lately had no note/ also has no comment on this latest development, but we've got the tiger by its tail. It folds its feet up like bat-wings. Its goes fur red, buff red, red gold, black under the whiskers, it submerges itself in a puff of·red smoke it slips from its ruffled sleeve. We extend the mechanical claw, we pocket its sere skull and sigh. Small wonder. As evidentiary record of ancient life, two pearls lump like apples in the back of a jeweled scaly snake. Rot in place like the eyes of the skate.

THE LEADER SPEAKS

—Flet, it's time to speak! We open our mouths like the birdie, for the birdie, we open our mouths like the cat that authored the canary, and what's for supper but a yellow feathery goo. Uh, wrong turn there, somewhere in the metaphor. Spit it out, start again, back to the square with the fountain and the tower. Square one. All lined up? Good. Start the tape. Begin again. In all cultures, Flet, there is a bird crowing, which represents the beginning of time, the dawn, the glorious clarion call that will be history starting over, erh, the second flowering, the second early dawn, the bonus round in the Skee-Ball match that with its din and thud ensembles life. Time to dawn, Flet. Time to din. Time to open that pretty bird-beak wide and throw the leather ball in. There's a clapper inside, a belt to vibrate, a ringtone, even a tongue to mash peas and vowels against the roof of that solemn mouth.

So all right, pet of mine. The pet scan assures us that the brain is functioning fine, making a lanyard of thoughts, firing on all cylinders, so the matter of speech is just a matter of time and a matter for you to decide.

Respondent: Clears throat.

—Good. I'll take that as an affirmation of my general line. Good then. Subverbal, surely, guttural, not unlike the crowing of some mud-brown frog in a brook, but audible, for all that, and therefore good. Good as an X on the dotted line. Let the record show: Subject cleared her throat. Now, Flet, in the month or so that you and I have been going about our limited business and growing fat as stoats, the world has not stood still, no it has not stood still one jot, groat, mote, or iote, tittle, dash, or smudge. It leers, it's complicating, a dire blow was struck, which needs no annotating for you, poor dear, you were right there on the ground for it, tut tut, for the worst of it. Yes?

Respondent (thinking): No. I didn't see it. I had no vantage. I missed both cause and effect. My back was turned on the whole thing. Maybe that's where the knowledge lies. Maybe that's where it's written.
(saying) (makes no note). (The silver swan/ that lately had no note)

—But we needn't press the matter, for though you were the only living body at that height, or low, you were not the only eye witness

Respondent's thought: or any eye witness

—Because the cameras of Nation were watching, dear girl, and caught it all in their retinal net. We have angle after angle already, we've studied the aggregate and brought ourselves into sickish intimacy with the crime, yes, the outrage against Nation. Another testimonial, in other words, is not what we need from you.

Respondent: expressionless.

—What we need from you, Flet, is to survive. We need a face of Nation. And not just a face. A carriage, a carapace, a mien, a bearing, a photo-portable demeanor. Do you begin to understand? Now: Your training with the Martyr Otis should have prepared you well for any duty your new position might ask you to perform. In fact your new position requires you only to be exactly as you were before. Unfazed. Unchanged. We've retrieved your clipboard. Unflappable. Adaptable. Still Flet. Still the Nation.

Respondent: (tears involuntary)

—You are not ready. I see. Still weak. Poor girl. Still I cannot say "poor child" because you are not quite that, Flet, and eventually you are going to have to give over this childish sulking and get on your two sturdy feet. But not yet, I see. Not yet. More rest is involved. I'll inform your auxiliary to administer a sedative and we can meet again later in the week. Guard! Despite this disappointing interview, Flet, I still believe you to be retrievable, capable of doing your duty to Nation. In short, still of use to the Administration and to me. So better focus our energy on pulling ourselves together, right? All smiles, next time. Guard! Take this from me.

INSIDE THE SKULL, INSIDE THE CELL

Chop, chop, and up. The ankle flexes, the tension remasters. How the body holds physics in its hold. The falangist medals, clanging at each other. Pig phalanx advances under a hill of skin. The boot sighs and weakens. The foot kicks. The sledge shifts. The ball soars. The pig skin. The net dissolves into wriggling larvae and silk chords. The risers betray their bolts and fall into an arguing racket. The turf rolls back; our colt remains suspended on an airy and weightless plane, a belly band is fastened to haul it up through a trapdoor punched in the stage of heaven, and then through its roof. The crystalline sphere rolls back for the burden. The eye of the colt flashes yellow, and as it rises it spins as if draining away in a flood.

Now it roams the Upper World peering through its own thick skull through time with inward eyes. The Upper World is multiplied, its gold and liquid vesicles, corridors, its lipids and orbitals, its vistas of clover and rye sprouting in the fissures that split the skull-plates, well in the pits. Occlusions and nebulae, this colt can lie down now/ among the cool pastures, in the spongy neural meadows of the mind.

The ambulance arrives and unhinges. Hinges open like the jaw of a bony dummy that opens organless, from gravity, not even a breath tucked in its slatted breast. In a moment's indecision, gravity wobbles, the clock-hands snap away and the clock-face is blank. Hinges open and clocks out.

GEOGRAPHER'S LOG

Today it happened! Our flip phones began blinking, our Administration-channel filescreens beamed maps and protocols, our printers rattled to life. After a month, it seemed, the Administration was ready to make use of us again! As the six of us sat in the middle of the whirring, banging room, how lucky we all felt to not have abandoned our habits of industry when it seemed so tempting to do so. But to be honest, I don't think any of us was ever tempted, much. Creatures of habit, as they say. Moles in our industrial-sized mole hill, we never fancied ourselves kings of any scale.

Of course without any staff or auxiliaries there was some improvisation as to who would receive and preview the dispatches, who organize and distribute them, and so forth. I volunteered to perform these tasks, which were easy, after all, if flustering. It was not unlike standing up in a rowboat and punting along with the oar. We soon managed well enough.

We work in the Bureau of Maps, which is overseen, ultimately, by the Continuous Heritage czar, unless you count God himself as the ultimate overseer. As young men, we were technicians, with our map-greens, washed blues and delicate buffs, red and black lines for routes and highways, crisp navy for currents, purple for elevations, precision gridlines, arguments about foreshortening and scale that could take up many afternoon's tea-breaks, T-squares and slide-rules and compasses and calculators and graphs and handmade glossed wooden cases with clasps and locks. Aerial photographs were one thing, but still had to be blocked and schematized for human consumption, and when the first satellite maps beamed back to earth earth itself in all its cloudy glamour, we were excited as schoolboys. But with each wrenching shift in perspective came a technological shift that bled down to the very strata where we dwelt. We became obsolescence, not just figuratively but literally embodied, six aging men in aging suits, reassigned to formulate protocol, approve letterhead and logos, and relay the Administration dispatches to the youthful, atomized technician-specialists below us in the chain: The Dynamic Block animators, the Automotive Cell, the Uplinkers, the Downloaders, the Education Media scriptors, and so forth. Most of our activities dwelt on erosive or topical changes brought about by natural or manmade events, from remote revolutions to remoter icepack dissolutions, the drying up of lakes and the crumbling of shorelines. Sometimes in the interest of national security we would remove a land or water route from all future editions of a map.

Do not misunderstand me: Ours is not an Orwellian enterprise. The fossil record of previous maps is not destroyed or altered in any way. It doesn't need to be. Who would order a defunct map? As obsolescence's children, ourselves, it is our job to oversee the obsolescence of charts and documents. In a way, we become the more artists for it, delivering these benighted labors of love—sometimes devised by our own hands!—into the eternity of beauty, no longer constrained by utility itself.

As for our own illustrative itches, you will think it silly, but those we secretly still pursue, or I do, and I suspect I am not the only one of us brothers that sits up late into the night, hand steadied by an iceless nightcap, redrafting the latest face of the Nation onto fresh paper, shading its renewing youthfulness, the blankness at its margins and its heart.

AUXILIARY VIEW: FILETAPE OF FLET

Testifying, today, is Flet's boss. She speaks directly into the camera, she has a perfect knife-blade bob that forms points around her chin, a mauve suit with a Chinese collar, a dazzling lotus-shaped brooch worked from a cluster of optical fibers. Her face is classically beautiful, regally aged, neatly made up, and, as she answers the questions she tilts her head slightly to one side, just as if she were alive. The sound has been turned off. Periodically her brooch gives off a glittery signature.

Frame by frame, her face is being eaten by a depthless green-black, which proposes a matterless declivity, a visible vacuum, in the shape of her shade and visage, poised before her microphone. Behind her Flet and a collection of auxiliaries and experts gaze on the proceedings with bland concentration.

Before the filescreen, Flet keeps a tight expression, sitting as erect and professionally bland as her mirror-self on the screen. At her side a single technician manipulates the filetape, completing the erasure of Secretary Otis and moving on to a collection of flunkies and dignitaries still visible in the frame. As face after face is clipped, blotted, and erased, Flet's own features remain lifelike on the screen, which wavers slightly under some pressure from a vent. It is like looking into clear water, this ripple effect.

The technician is building one of a series of templates for the Continuous Heritage database; as visual protocol is being refined and finalized, a model is required that animators across the Administration can consult for the staging of future events. To simply use the templates, editing in one or two live agents, is easier and safer than to convene a meeting of the governing remnant, currently sequestered in far-flung compounds and even under mountains and large rocks. Since so many variant lists exist, it is proving surprisingly difficult to determine which administrators and staffers appear in any given piece of filetape, let alone which, due to their unfortunate recent demise, should be removed from future templates. Since no technician can be expected to know every face on sight, this editing and animation process involves exhaustive cross-checking and repetition of labor. Today's session is no less tedious: Having combed carefully through the throng of Flet's colleagues and peers, the technician now alternately removes and restores glares, shadows, and shadings, to approximate the ways in which light strikes and sinks away in a space emptied of bodies.

Flet excuses herself and exits the cell. She walks down the corridor, leans on the heavy metal crossbar and pushes open the door in front of her. As she has shown herself capable of what is required of her, she has been given as much liberty as she cares to consume, to walk the corridors or the dusty few feet of open space between the buildings. She is struck by how mnemonic sensation is now, how familiar the heavy weight of sunlight against her suit shoulders, the stress on her ankles of the unevenly packed walks. In these floating afternoons, she has the double sensation of walking forward and walking in place. Yet the line between then and now is narrow and absolute. She carries it with her, straight and exact as the shaft of an arrow lodged in her back.

Tonight she has a dream in her flickering green chamber, an unusual dream that begins entirely as an odor, a sweet, heavy, concentrated fragrance that unwinds her from her bed and reels her down the corridor and out into the night-light, that is to say, into night's dream double, lit from above in a powdery white beam. She hears a beating and a motor and a wind hurled, as if from a hovering helicopter, and the powdery static light soon coats her throat. She momentarily loses the scent of the scent, but then she regains it, the heavy fragrance laying across her cheeks like a welcome, obscuring mask. Then beam and noise lift away and she's in darkness. She crosses the empty courtyard, slips into a passageway between buildings to the left and walks along, her left hand following the brick of the building. She reaches the corner and turns left into a blank well. There, casting its own dim vegetable light from a cheap green plastic pail, is a heavy, blossoming bush, which rustles slightly, shakes its almost visible fragrance from its red wax petals, straightens again, shies coquettishly and pulls its petals over itself, then grins and straightens up boldly for her gaze. Flet keeps one hand in contact with the building but leans closer. Abruptly the white, alienating light snaps on once again from above, flooding the scene with powder and static. The bush begins shaking, even convulsing, until Flet becomes terrified that it will shred apart and some vicious animal or other living thing will eat its way out of the bush's destroyed innards. But as the noise and light begins to subside, these seizings become regular, until the dense bush is no longer convulsing but pulsing calmly. Flet snaps her head back and finds herself looking not into the retreating runners of a helicopter but into a mass of red glistening tissue hovering and beating just a few feet from her face. Then it lifts away, turning as it rises, dragging its blinking, light-tipped arteries in its wake. As the distance doubles between them, Flet wills herself in vain to see farther, into the bladed, withdrawing thing, the night-erasing heart.

INSIDE THE SKULL, INSIDE THE CELL

The hemicircular table again and again until the hall is a phalanx: full. On animatronic necks, curious machineries lower to nuzzle the line. Deep in the gut, ruptured tissue reclads itself until the bursting wall protrudes. A knot in which the first wound sleeps and steeps. On the forward wall, a gold plaque thick with gloss, where each face turns to find itself reflected. On the plaque, a netted globe, a plump prize or exemplum.

On the interior lid of the assembly plant, a spider spans the girders. At seafloor-level, clustered cephalopods are at work. Each delegation struggles to print black figures on a card. Each votive, vote, denial, or resolution is passed with a raising of cards, which the spider lowers herself to graze. She digests only the scrawled letters and vomits a pap of cards in a tensile paste she strings from plinth to plinth. The lid grows more and more elaborately wrought. There are more and more queer redoubts and recesses into which the assembly peers. The cephalopods duck their foot-heads and shudder, bilaterally; candles snuff out, then reconsider and come around. The seafloor spreads and sighs. It is covered in sugar frosting. When the machines miss and shoot bolts into the ground, these are entirely buffered. No one is harmed. In free hours, the spider improves the net in which the world is caught.

At breakout, a golden gavel sinks like a sun, a midnight shade drops down to cover the netted world, the cephalopods gather themselves into their shells or mantles of tissue and prepare to leave the hall. They have read of themselves that they are the most intelligent invertebrates, and they believe it, hurling their body masses backwards over the floor to withdraw into their colorblind libraries of tones. But when the lights of the plant are dark, the spider is alone and alive. She inverts herself, performs the swing shift, sings each passage of the elaborating text.

GEOGRAPHER'S LOG

It is strange, now that our life has resumed its previous rhythm of constantly arriving and departing missives, reams of paper converted from digital blips and reconverted to electric signals, that the return of our precious status quo once seemed so desirable to us. To be sure, it is easier now to pass away, say, two-thirds of our workday with meetings and tasks, as opposed to the one-third day's makework we were able to manufacture during our period of total lockdown. But in the end there is just as much emptiness in being the living conduit in an elaborate switching machine, merely adding our patina of rhetoric to the plastic-clad directive as it courses on, as in feeling cut from this process, adrift in our orange vinyl visitor's chairs, as we were through those first lonely weeks.

The mood in the morning meetings, on the other hand, has greatly improved, now that we have our sense of purpose about us. Just last week, Chu, the youngest among us, abruptly brought it to our attention that it was a Friday, and that if we were going to remain sequestered at this plant for much longer we should start to claim the normal human rhythms to which we were entitled. We agreed to meet at five that evening to toast the sunset from the rooftop viewing area I call the parapet.

But I finished cross-checking the week's task list against confirmed results with several hours to spare, and took to my feet as usual, my dress shoes resounding in the high-glossed tile hallways, wingtips kicking up streaks and threads of emergency light. In the pith of my automatic motion, I proposed to myself the task of retrieving my filetape screen from the long-abandoned convalescent's quarters. Yet when I reached the room, rather than the decisive action I had envisioned, I merely found my whole body melting, yes, sinking with an enervation which could perhaps be explained by the slightly stuffy quarters, the late afternoon hour, the fact that I am no longer as young as Walker, let alone Chu. I lowered myself as lightly as possible onto the cot, intending to rest just a minute, then stretched myself out to full length, my heels and shoes hanging off the end. In truth this cot was not entirely comfortable, with its tough vinyl surface, all sheeting and blanketing having been removed by the auxiliary. I sat up, folded my jacket under my head, and switched on the filescreen, tuning to Informed Electorate, mindful that it was still working hours, somewhere outside and up above.

And then I saw her, as I have at this hour of every day since. Did it surprise me, or was my life so reduced to a handful of variables that it seemed only right that she should reappear to me, in a minutes-long vignette? The spot began with file footage of the neat, youthful girl going about her pre-catastrophic duties, accompanying that female education official on tours of various facilities and sitting among her peers at hearings and functions. Next, the screen went to white, followed by a sequence of her sitting alone at these same venues. Turning a grave yet resolute eye on the camera as it zoomed out to the far corners of the darkened and colossal hall, providing, as it were, the vantage of a spider or a bat, the doll-like figure voiced the object of this object lesson: Courage makes us Still the Nation.

Or she appeared to voice it. The decision to zoom out rather than in during this tagline, to position her amidst the vastness of the hall rather than emphasize the human portal of her human eye, was a queer one. Geographers are connoisseurs of scale, and I puzzled over this choice, the way the girl seemed to shrink away from me at the end of every airing. Why those orchestrating the piece chose not to represent the girl's rescue by the intrepid Catastrophic Response Team driver, or her long, silent recovery in our own compound, is more thinkable. The urgency of her wasted, animaline visage would have represented an unknown element in the rhetorical calculation of the whole. Raw, inhuman desperation can be difficult to consume, and its effects on the digesting public may vary by individual.

I turned these matters over as I climbed the mathematically veering staircase to the parapet. I emerged through the final white-painted door, which was habitually covered on both sides with some fine grit. There I found my cólleagues, plump and flushed as children in their dark suits, handing around gold starburst glasses that had been retrieved from one or another lounge or cabinet, and pouring out gin-and-tonics perfumed with an artificial lemon tincture. All around them, beyond the parapet, evening held up impossibly brilliant panels of saffron, orange, and gold, soaring and pressing close, so thick was the precipitate in the air, refracting the light. It was like standing in a votive flame, or a Venetian dish, a sweet experience, and a happy gratitude filled me bodily, though gratitude towards what I could not have said.

Since that day I've amended my original plan and, rather than retrieving my filescreen, return to the deep chamber every day to watch this airing, and, sometimes again in the evening, raise my glass in salute and as a kind of lens to reverse the girl's withdrawal into the crushing vanishing point of the final scene. One drowsy afternoon, close to sleep, or perhaps having crossed into sleeping, I felt the darkness around me form a kind of body and reach out to touch the darkness in which the girl herself was consumed, and form one long, living, lightless substance. I slept in earnest in that womb, feeling I had at last unlocked the unspoken logic of the program's queer dimensions.

AUXILIARY VIEW: A REELING

Now she is reeling. There are probably three. Three falls, three flights. When she reaches into a slung coat for a key and feels its teeth in her fingers, many teeth in this pocket, she carries off the lot like something living, bunched in her palm. This is the way to begin. When she swats the sensor pad with her elbow, the camera stops and curls around to purr as she walks under, lifting her own gaze to meet its blank, reflective eye. This is the way to walk out. When she crosses the tar lot lit for symbolism's sake, she finds the auxiliary's much-bragged-about knifeblackmuscletang parked in the far dark corner of the lot. She hits the button on the side of the key ring and a lewd anthem tinkles wanly, traveling no farther than the six inches between herself and the car. Just now light drops weightlessly from the canopy of dead stars and frays out thousands of feet above the canopy of kliegs. Inside the car, the mechanism relents dimly; she draws a breath, then seizes the handle, opens the door, and climbs inside in one motion. She has never driven a car like this, brought in from Nation B on a system of bilge-vomiting barges, and hopes they don't take much driving. She turns the key and the dash lights up with vernal symbols. She finds a button for driver setting, cycles from 'AUX. BILL' to 'NEW DRIVER,' and feels the seat embrace her and scoot her, intimately, closer to the controls. Then, hoping that the car will not make any further chintzy or fevered external signs to the world at large, or send warning to AUX.BILL asleep in front of the filescreen, she shifts gears, touches her foot to the gas, and drives as steadily as possible out of the lot.

Out on the highway, she drives for eight minutes at ever increasing speeds alongside a length of razor-topped chain-link protecting nothing she can see from the road. Then she lifts her foot from the gas and lets the car glide to a stop, a woman's voice reading out her declining speed in worried, five mile increments, diamonds in the fence breaking from their blur like startled cows to face her one-on-one, one by one. Flet rests her cheek on the headrest and studies the linear shape of one diamond, cannot quite make out from this distance how it twists and becomes the next. She drives on slowly, but no landmarks come into view, no lights, not even any turnoffs from this road. She realizes more palpably than ever that she does not know where she is. She punches a button and a sterile ditty floods the compartment like lukewarm juice: *your heart, my flag, the rain, my tears, this war, our fears, came true, I'm blue, goddang.* I'm blue goddang, I'm blue goddang. In my stolen muscletang, Flet rewrites these words as the synth twang flies. Then she punches the music out. When she glances down again to catch the time, she sees that the dash display is scrambled. She can't see the shoulder, stops instead in the middle of the road. A system of variegated points reaches within itself on pin-sized axels. After a few moments, Flet realizes she is looking at a constellation of satellites, chunky as nuts and bolts, cycling on the other side of the haze. She touches the display and it converts, this time to a strip of blackness floating in a sea of green. This, then is the road, featureless, a seam through a featureless dream. Looking from the display to the smear of light coating the hood of the car, Flet sees the ground fall away, the capsule rising, floating, dislodged. The car flips around, then flips again. Flet closes her eyes, grips the steering wheel hard, and feels the car settle and ground. She taps the screen one more time, and a map zooms out, she can see herself as a blinking star halfway between a rectangle labeled 'WORK' and a notch in the coast Flet knows to be the site of the ferry slip below Near Cliff. She taps the screen again, but instead of zooming closer it resets, gives her the same picture but with a blurring of the keyhole notch in the coastline she feels she has known her whole life. She puts her fingertips to her eyes, then looks again. Now the map recenters, but with the coastline swept angular and clean, no declivity marking the spot where the Re-Enactment bit a hole in the sweep of things. She stares expressionlessly at this, then out at the vague declivity all around her. And then she puts her forehead to the steering wheel and begins to cry. With each heaving sob against the wheel, the straps of her seatbelt push back at her shoulders and torso, until her own emotion and this nylon contraption form a dyad, a closed system, locating itself again and again in the universe, a logicless call and response. When she is exhausted, and aching, she pulls herself up in her seat. The straps loosen and release her into conversation with the rest of the world. She wheels the car around and makes her way back to the compound.

In the parking lot, she punches up the settings for 'AUX.BILL' and hopes the car's computers will erase all signs of her. Back in the low halls, green like the veins of some synthetic leaf or anesthetized monster, she heads for the breakroom and deposits the keys casually among the coffee cups and styrofoam trays strewn on the table where the auxiliary will certainly look for them when he finds them missing. Then she returns to her own cell and sits down stiffly on the bed, her back to the wall. She closes her eyes; her joints ache with tension. Her body struggles to catch and sort the new data coursing through.

INSIDE THE CELL, INSIDE THE SKULL

The tronke jampacked   with goods for her jorney
she finds expansive   : that place could holde
as much as two armies   two arms and optics.
Could fit her forme.   Fill a caske
Of light yeares   with burdrennes. Lost
ligaments and Polaroides   of polar lite,
litoral smeares of   selvage and muddle,
womb of galaxies   warping the glossed
pages ripped   from bio preps.
A geographie of knowledge   knowne by harte
trayced in the mind   like the teeth of a keye.
A bay, a locke,   a slip and a lippe
of lande fit   for a ferrye landing.
A shallow field   and a shunned deserte.
A craytered lake   for a craythur to gayze
on life opening   without her mien
to mint; no double   her in its depths
but invert mountains to valleyes. All
these coeval shapes   that start and end
with her, discarded.   A dense strip
of words like stroking   the wilde hare
to calm its harte.   Such useless codes
and spent languages   lately tossed
into her tronke. Family   feeling and truste.
What the bodey   wakes for. All fits.
She slammes the lid   and spies the shield
which though transparent   is tempered strong,
and there her visage   and torso veer
stretched and shield-like, her forehead a shield,
she's vouchsafed by selfhood. Passage
and means of passage: her own mete machine.
She lokes the carre   and leaves it in the lot
and·she swallows it down   and carries it away
and also always   she dwells inside it,
posed among the mirrors   that hide her mug
from view, eclipsed   in their curved vantage.
Now how could one thing   at once be three:
container, contained   and accessorie? This
hard riddle   hies like a hare
from my thatched hutch   into thine hands.

GEOGRAPHER'S LOG

When, precisely, the girl disappeared is a complicated question. When she disappeared from the telecasts?—never. The unmarked file footage spooled on in the timelessness of the darkened halls, the polished, nearly painted-on gleams that kissed the water glass, the gleaming teeth, the podia and wristwatch, the sheen that floated over the entire proceedings as if one gazed into the thick-lensed televisions of our youth and not this treated, sheetlike screen. But I noticed—for I had become a habitual fan and follower of her appearances, reviewing in pooled darkness her daily ritual presences at the grief ceremonies and software hearings—a certain cycling and recycling of her images, a point at which no novel tableaux rose to the surface of the screen. For some nights I wondered if I were just misfiring the controls, if within some fillip of code hid a pixilated nook or cranny, a whole new animated landscape unfolding on an infinitesimal—and thus infinite—scale. But instinct finally told me otherwise. I sensed that the girl was no longer available to be taped.

Where are we, when we can no longer be recorded? For weeks of nights I had splayed myself before this display, this failed interface, where I could look on her image but not be touched by it, the light reaching me from the filetape screen as remote from her as starlight from a star—no, more remote, because it had never touched or withdrawn from her face. And now I was stricken by this awareness that she was not in that place, was no place this screen could reveal to me. I got up from the cot and made, at first, by instinct, to the rooftop parapet. But as I set my hand on the push-bar that would open the door to the staircase, the familiarity of its grooved surface gave me pause. Here was a door I had touched so many times, a sensation I had so often dwelt in, I could withdraw to my chamber right now and make, from memory, a map of this metal's flaws and striations, inset with a nerve map from my palm to my cortex. Over a series of coded pages I could render the collapsible quadrants of the stairsteps, the parapet above, a nestling troposphere and even a celestial map above that. But what would be beyond this sensible space? What would be outside it?

I resolved to collect this data. My first job was to find a door to the outside. I had been in this plant for so long, scuttling like a one-clawed crab across its layers, that I was no longer sure how I had entered the compound. But I did recall that posted next to one odd closet in a far corner of the lower basement was a boxy map hand-drawn on a piece of paper. It took me, you will believe, some hours to relocate this very corner of the basement, hours of wandering in the mazelike interstices of identical green tiles, suspended lighting, flat gray doors. Once I had the map before me it took an instant to master its simple schematic, its in-case-of-fire dashed red-markered line bleeding directly towards the pie-shaped doors that were, in this rendering, standing open for just such events. I slotted down the spindly halls and in no time found myself before one of the ancient, gunmetal grey slabs hung before the advent of the alarmed exit but posing the danger of being potentially locked or rusted shut. Consciously driving a hesitating energy back into the gut-level duct from which it rose, I put my shoulder to the door and hove, with all the power of an old man wrenching unspent strength from the deep reserves of his youth.

The door did more than glide open: it flew; I lost my feet; I found myself airborne, suspended as if by Surprise herself, and then falling, nearly prone, to a collection of pains which varied and remapped my body in the utter dark. A round scraping pain circled the heel of my left palm and leapt up my wrist at intervals. Both knees smarted boxily but felt more badly drawn than badly damaged. Most worryingly, a pain shot from my mandible to the base of my skull, redrawing the route along which my skull did snap back when I collided with what felt like asphalt carpeted in a tough, virile grass. I got to my knees and one palm, my blood and nerves and incredible chemicals carrying news of the fall all around my alert and aching body. If I had expected to find myself in a parameterless atmosphere, some insensible materia like sleep which would again connect me to the girl, I was utterly mistaken.

I settled on my haunches and peered out. The darkness was nearly total; no security lights blurred from above me, though I was fairly certain that by following the wall I could find my way back to the lit realm. I got to my feet, and, steadying myself as well as possible, turned my head very slowly through its one-hundred-and-eighty measly degrees, trying to detect any alteration in the seamless fabric that hung thickly around me. On my third or fourth sweep I detected a red pinpoint of light, tiny, which, as I began to move, tentatively, toward it, grew no larger but turned on its narrow end, a thread that drew me away from terra firma and into an incognita, that sought to thread the eye of me, or that, some dull part of me knew, sought only to complete itself, and, unable to do so because of my intervening form, was furiously signaling an alarmed receptor, which might soon bring the whole night down around me.

INSIDE THE CELL, INSIDE THE SKULL

This was information: tilted in the breathing darkness like fault-shuffled graves around a swiveling pinion, a cluster of stars growing closer, lines closing a kite or box, a robed lady withdrawing on sandaled feet across the universe, her palm held up above the floodwaters, the tide to her knees, the tide to her thighs, the fabric darkening, hiccupping, entangling her, blossoming sisters clinging in a wreath to the neck of an ox, a bow flexed, a torso flexed for hunting or tearing the sky down, a secreting of shadows into a blue period. Crack the whip. Saltimbanque. Tricorner hat of time. For you are the salt of the earth, and when salt has lost its slaver, what then? A rabid yellow dog jiving in the courtyard. He does the shimmy and he does the shake. Yea, but he fears the slake. Long hair waves and tangles across the map. Dishy and mystical, it blinds the eyes. We arrived at the lake, and found it salt. We arrived at the salt, and found it God. We arrived at the ocean, and found it rampant. String the lyre. Rescue by dolphins. Dip in the Styx. Torn apart by angry ladies like a racecar hitting the wall. Here are the whitewalls that were his eyes. Stopped at the red light; poised for the hit man; eyes rolling back in the SUV. The sclerotic veil revolving and eclipsing like a half-blank disco ball. For when the eye has lost its slaver, what then? Blind man, by your sense of the sea, steer the vessel. Lift the staff. Part the water. Strange fruit swings in stormy welter. Waxwings. The storm at sea. Wax lips and jelly babies. Learning, the barefoot boys in straw hats before the red schoolhouse. Leaning. Instruction: the beaming bush. These pajamas inflammable according to the laws of California. I cannot tell a lie, except to a pieman. I cannot tell a secret, except from a hole in the ground.

An Optic Parable

A young woman dipped a bucket into a well. She pulled up a liquid limpid as the eye's humor. She filled a glass bowl, and raised it with two hands to eye level. Her arms strained under the weight. Through this heavy lens, she looked on a rabid cur, currently swirling in the foot of shadow that clung to the base of a wall. He spun again and again as if to lie down for his rest, but he never lay down. She could make out every raised hackle, every bristle tipped with saliva, the cut nostrils and the fangs and the fang-white eye each time the beast spun around. She set the bowl on the ground at the side of the well and walked backwards away from the animal, her arms still raised by reflex to her face. The dog stopped and turned itself in her direction. The girl's muscles locked. As the dog launched himself towards her she scrambled up onto the lip of the well, steadying her sandal's soles on the wide stone facing. Kicked away, the bowl skittered and shattered to one side. The dog circled the well, snapping and snarling at her feet as he went 'round, and at first she craned her neck so that she would always have the animal in her sightlines. But soon she was worried that she would lose her balance this way and tumble into the well. She moved her heels as close as possible to the inner rim and shut her eyes; then, wobbling, she opened them again and tried to focus on the lower corner of a window opposite. Steady. The dog began throwing himself at the well, at times knocking his skull against the stone and falling with a human exhalation to the dust before snapping upright as if shocked alive and returning to his endeavor; and at times just clearing the top of the well with his jaws, till she could sense the heat of his slaver at the edges of her soles. Suddenly, there was another commotion in the yard, and two men with clubs and one with a spear rushed close to subdue the dog, circling as he circled, or turning against his current, lunging and leaping back clear of the snapping jaws. The dog became almost two-headed in these dual pursuits, lunging at the circling girl and answering the jabs of the circling men.

What a system this was, they would marvel later, what a model of time. And how strange that she never made a noise until the exact moment the spear-point, aimed for his neck, instead found the cur's belly, as his fang-points finally made headway in the bridge of her foot.

AN OPTIC PARABLE

Poised over the gleaming console, our young woman taps a pad that bends an articulated wrist and waves a sensor over a well. The monitor jumps with information, casts up an index acid-green as a warrior's eye misting with death or envy. The console beeps back. She presses a control and lowers a lens over the shield of the craft. The scene swells and jumps closer. Through this heavier vision, she examines bacterial mats, thick, autumn-hued florescences, crusts and chimneys, cones and domed protuberances leafing over the vent. Here is resourcefulness, fecundity, proximity, knowledge shared through nearness, inseparability, a beginning again. Reader, though her basket is empty, her coring tool ready for the descent, she is reluctant to take her sample. Reader, though crew members await on the surface vessel, she is reluctant to take her leave, reader that she is, of the smoking flow and streaming essence of the seafloor. She hovers over the page, clicking with information. Wrapped in syntactic foam, buoyant cladding forged at the cereal factory from the same generative molds as would forge the cereal machines, serially, prior to the flakes, malt, and generative molds of grainy contact, prior to oceanic descent; and now, the balance tipped, she's jumped the spirit level, she's sunk into aftermath, to where she holds her depth. In the bubble hull, she rests in vacant space, content to settle for meaning, the content meant for settling.

Far above, elsewhere and indubitably monitored, a flat-backed brown caterpillar struggles in a distance-colored thread, its effortful spinning only tightening the web. This spinning slows. This beast is tens of times larger than the antic spider that waits in a crack for poison or exhaustion to effect its quarry. Knitting its own shroud, the caterpillar is incompletely clad; now its feelers and tubules stroke the air for information; brainlessly intellectual, it wants to know how this conversion from freedom to capture has been arranged, what element doubled and doubled over to fold this crawling beast into the past tense of the day. Into the benighted column. If a hand or twig should free it, this creature would only pause on the ledge and with slow aching motions turn itself back again, into the web, which hangs like a mirage of ghostly rockface or necrotizing cancer under the resonant lens. Once the slow beast has enmeshed itself again, the monitor spider emerges from its shelf and bastes it into place. Day loses attention for the long race.

The woman turns off her spot, but it is impossible to turn off all the monitors and eyelights of the nest in which she sits. She flips her spot back on and the crenellated, motley cloth again spreads before her like a map of her own brain. Always with her, just behind her eyes, its topological districts and reserves, its mysterious veiled wells and resources. With a flick of her fingers, she lowers the coring tool into the mass.

AUXILIARY VIEW

Flet hunkers in the metastasizing night. She knows how information spreads, where it is bred, in the heart and in the head, on diodes and parts per million, in matching caskets of gold, silver, and lead, draining here, blistering elsewhere, bottled up at its most fragrant, beestung and removéd Belmont. It bends with the remover to remove, and is removed, packed in the logoless white van, this drive wiped, this quadrant smoothed from the face of the map.

Build, honeybees, the bildungsroman of this now. With your gilt guild, your hive marked vincit, your sash and your racket which evinces industrie.

Every nerve in the fabric is firing. The night is dim and clear. A belt of pearls is hanging from the waist of night. Flet's pupils dilate to gather the image, flip it in their mirrors, and change it to information. We are one-third into the lifecyle of this thought, which will last another two million years. Communication well. Communicate well, moth star. Gap traveler.

Another mile or two back, Flet jumped the roadster over the gravel shoulder and into the weedy gullet at its side. The impact was greater than she'd expected, perhaps because of her speed when she left the road; she awoke some time later with a wrenched neck and a stung forehead thrown back. It was difficult to remember her checklist then as she extricated herself from the body of the car, to locate the backpack she'd stowed in the seat behind her, to hook its strap with her wrist, to maneuver the sprained door and the entangling belt angled across the whole opening, then to choose whether to walk out of sight in the gulley or up on the road. Under its black cloak of weeds, the gulley shrugged and squirmed away from her at unexpected moments, causing her ankle to buckle and her thinking to go even more webbed and woozy, so she clambered up on the hardtop and took to the middle of the road. Its reflective seam clarified. The whole night could fold there. It stretched to both sides without distinction. No emergency sirens bruised the darkness, no unmarked tires made a path for her, to scoop her up or knock her from the road. Her head was not clearing, though with effort she straightened her back, forced her breathing and her gait to slow, and when she reached the lot of dim low structures she remembered, she remembered to lift her knees high so as not to catch her shins on the chain.

Now she sits with her back against the stucco, which holds warmth from the day, feels wrought from cakes of accumulated dust. Seated in the dustscape, now the road disappears. Before her a constellation bleeds through the sky; behind her she recalls the clearer constellation, the racks of two-toned placid maps and ripe postcard images, the shelves of unnatural and preserved foods shrinking in their wrap. She and Mick had stopped so briefly here, yet if she had a lit cigarette or a laser pen she could draw on the vagueness before her a star chart of what's behind her, minute quadrants, its contents and wells and depths. The map, laid out in red, is too much to hold in the mind, and like sparks it fades ashily. What's before her, what's alive in the furl of the night, through what membrane instinct and intuition seep and code, banks deliciously against the prow of her consciousness, the rich and expectant present tone, harmony, a bowl she is filling, a prow that dissolves, a brow that is bruised and a pulse that signals like a radio tower back at its own responsive heart.

GEOGRAPHER'S LOG

When I awoke it was early dawn, silver-gilt as if by some mawkish Victorian method for casting keepsakes and souvenirs. The strange materia, which felt riven with grit, a ductile particulate, covered my skin and the aluminum fence-post one shoulder was driven against, coated my thighs through my trousers. I coughed, and felt it cover my tongue. Clambering up, I could feel ropy organics under my shoes and metal rhomboids at my back and stretching over my head and to either side, filling arms' reach. I could see only cubic feet in front of me, and these were filled with the uncanny, scentless fog. At least the presence of the presumed fence cut axes in my limitless options. I could go left or I could go right, or I could walk away from the fence and into a cloud of unknowing, or I could turn my face into the fence and feel time and distance part and extend around the new universal central point where my body met the uniform metal. I looked down through the fog at my shirtsleeves. Where it touched my body the fog was mere heavy moisture, did not leave a streak of tinning on my clothes or on my flesh. But the touch of it was so thick, so chilling, I felt my properties had changed. I had become a tin man, or was it tinned. Was I meant to skip pleasantly on a gold-plated road all the way to a toxic, repellant, trinitite city, or was I meant to lie fish-scaled among my scalar brothers dreaming open-eyed through my superhuman shelf-life, through generations and nuclear wars under a tin blanket weighed in place with a key.

Dextrous, I chose right, what difference did it make, and began to slog through the upright marsh of the half-morning, with one hand bitten by tooth after tooth in the cheaply clad fence. It created a cumulative fizzing effect, and my hand carried the motion even when it hung at my side filling heavily with the buzzy pulse that belonged there. I would say I walked but the motion was more repetitive than cumulative, so, more aptly, I stepped and stepped again, sometimes bringing my two feet together like a child climbing a stair before stepping further. I tried to search in my mind for the missing folly that would unite the other follies in this sequence into some shape like causality, remembered tripping through the door, crawling on my knees, espying the red needling light ahead of me. But the intervening chapters were lost. I was stuck here, marooned in silverplate, in collodion, promising my own image into every frame in the reel, but unable to see what all this Muybridging amounted to. What attitude of man did I represent, and who was studying me.

I was able to note, after some span of time, a lightening of the mist around me, and then a burning that found my scalp somehow amid all the depths of the morning and the bones of my wrists and any other protuberance that broke the surface of me. And then almost at once the whole veil lifted away. What had seemed a constant state in which I would march on, Learlike, forever, was wiped away instantly and a new realization set in: that I was along the outer walls of our own compound; that I could see the gate from here, and, before me, through the rhomboid fence, the rises of our own parapet. I am not sure how far I had come from where I originally broke the building's seal, or how I had found myself on the wrong side of this fencing, but the story in sum was, I had not come far. With my muscles aching and palms, I now realized, sore and scabbed, limping from the gate to the nearest portal of the building, I entered the omnifamiliar cool green corridors, and returned myself to a scene that seemed set before my headlong departure from the plant, my capsule life here impervious to the loop of events that had deranged and endangered me over the previous twelve or so hours. I walked, aching, backwards in time, making for my chamber. I was bodily marked by what had befallen me, or what I had befallen, but time itself, or at least time inside this compound, was not. I cast a glance on the scalding digital readout of the clock; I would not even miss our morning meeting.

INSIDE THE SKULL, INSIDE THE CELL

Light glare on the morning meeting. Binder laminate, floating cream-clot, Camelot, among the dunes, self-dissolving sugar substitute, universal motion of the red stirrer, bread of ink at the mouth of the ballpoint, punctured wingtip, struck tone, electrons following one another through the overhead chutes and circuits, reflex singing from stem to wrist. *Stir stir stir.* Edenic I-beams shift like snoozing duenna beyond the drywall. Paper is thumbed and smoothed. Pixels flash and split on the filescreen. Peaceful chemistry.

Outside light lifts itself from its million metallic particlettes coating human structures and reassembles into the beams, troughs, trusses, pipes, clerestories, sheets, welded plates, and splayed, domed, or staggering roofs suspended daily over this valley.

Beyond the highway, beyond the map, light splits again, though whether it intensifies or becomes devitalized, sapped of its own complexity and turned to something harsh and singular is hard to say. Light is general over the dusty highway, the graveled throat of the gulleys, the punctured gut of the muscletang, the rotting metal signs that hang like busted clavicles from the splintering metal stanchions, the silver-clad ice bins that warp into canine attitudes, loyal but miserable, beside abandoned gas stations. If it fastens on a drop of dew here, catches the fray of dirt from the hind legs of a tiny rodent returning to its burrow, or is closed inside the cloistered interiors of a devout, spine-mantled saguaro, it keeps this worldly knowledge to itself. Indifferently, terribly, stirring occasionally as if in sleep or blown by breeze on a line, it rests its whole weight on the chemically cracked floor of the desert, from zenith to azimuth, fore to hind.

Over this flatness, her progress is swollen, nebulous, lotus, a bloom of limbs that involutes, occludes, and stretches, bone white, pitching along and straying back, a cloud motion, accruing and raining and duckling its own shallows, mounting and rising again on ethereal inklings and ankles. Instinct and arrows. At times flashing multiple as a sheath or sheaf of white deer or clutch of white mares shifting and bucking or white flyers spiraling on a storm and falling to coat wet pavements. White doves. Infectious pigeons. A current of relations. A channel of afterthought. Moves calmly through light's pylons and resistances, loses and recoups herself, sifts tenderly through hard surfaces. Falls like rays. Benevolences. Tends. Coaxes and coats. Exists. Thinks upwards through the viscous head of sky.

AUXILIARY VIEW

Flet is a wonder. Rather than reduced, she has become broad and long, an architecture of leg-bone and tarsal drawing itself out from any vanishing point. A theory and its proof. A sentient fabric, she pauses and waves, unpinned from the line of time. When she lies in place, breast to the earth or to a swell of breeze, she feels her neck lengthening, her jaw growing infinitesimally longer, making a place for a sharp rind of tooth to shake off vestigiality and rise through the bone. She flexes her corded back, and a smear of brilliant iridizing color furls up around and behind her, flicking just into the corners of her vision. But whether this is happening in the past or future, featherine or gasoline, she can't determine. She makes a sand noise deep in her throat, it grates against her neckbone. She riffles three fingers experimentally at the end of her bowed arms for the pleasure of sensing their muscled toughness, thick as talons. But her back limbs feel loose, as if they could braid together. Her eyes are perfect circles where the sun has touched them, their sockets decorated with a ring of sharp holes. She turns her head to one side, another. She lies on the rock. She practices falling through the rock, Icarine, an object lesson. Then the rock dissolves and she picks herself up.

Through the thick-gauge grasses at the knick of the road, she drags and hops. It is a labored ambulation, a visual rhythmic pattern now lateral, now vertical like a musical score. Now optical, now visceral. As she lurches forward and sways slightly back, her tail, a rudder, knifes in her wake, lashes and frets into any number of glyphs and punctuations, marking accents and carats, quotes and speculations, over the fuddled tongues of the grass. It is a readerless system that texts itself into being, texts static at the cooking air and rays slicing down to the former soil. The anthropic principle says that the universe is the one that allows for those here to perceive it, to perceive it. The multiverse holds up all possible cosmologies like a flute of champagne to the light; each bubble a potential biosphere. That dog won't fight. That flute won't play. That flue won't light. That sweep slouches home to his hole in the ground. F-stop. Shot. The *norske familiebjok* lies closed and extinct on the desk, and in it riffle the thick flight feathers of the archaeopteryx, iron-routed, dreaming of flying off the page to be singed in the gaslight of the close parlor. But the binding holds. What, then, does the archaeopteric principle hold, those burnt-out, perfected eyes in rock that set one glance, that set one piece of type at a time? That's what an instant is: it stands, and does not fall, though the scanner moves on, reading each price code. The instant spends eternity gazing down its own infinite and infinitesimal sightline, its singular confection, its crystal ball or hall.

Sun does not definitively descend or climb over Flet, or if it does, it cross-references so many identical vectors of *prior* and *since* that its motion loses distinction. Each moment for Flet is a dazzle of mica in the far flank of the road, the companionship of her own clawed foot or bristling shoulder suddenly shoving itself into her fixed plane of vision. In some time she arrives at a brazen shrine of the desert, plate glass schismed in a door frame that hangs in a flat-roofed, formerly milk-blue, curdled exterior. She hops among the shards, among the sharded shadow, to an array of wrappers and foils that glint in the murk of the interior, streaks of chocolate or glittering bits of salt she can smell from here. A chaotic distress about the place. She leaps to plastic register keys, the drawer shunts open on empty guts, she leaps to the top of a rack that spins decenteredly under her weight, and a feathery sheaf of maps bends and ruches the air as the contraption descants lazily before cluttering to the ground. Before it crashes, she leaps away, and rises in the same shape of sound. Nothing to eat here; the place has been thoroughly razed by what clawed or shambling foot before her, like her own. Perhaps her own.

She pulls the shadows around her and degrades for a while. Then the dark goes seamless and she practices her fall.

THE LEADER SPEAKS

Citizens of Nation. Tap. Tap. Is this on? Ahem.

Citizens of Nation. Oh, this button here? How about now. Hear me?

Citizens of Nation. I apologize for the technical interference which still besmirches our interface. You may blame the terrible events of Re-Enactment Day for this remaining lack of clarity on the registers and fibers and fiberwrack. An infinitesimal fraction of the total conductive surface, I assure you. Other than this we see each other clearly, do we not? You see me, and I, most assuredly, see each of you.

Some of you, the most estimable in age, may recall a time in the distant past when one could go without worry to spend an evening at a commercial eating establishment. The purpose of such trips was to give some shape to the workweek or disburse oneself of the papery money which despite its known health risks was still in circulation then, and which tended to collect around oneself like sighing, worn-smooth leaves. On such an evening, breezy and autumnal or wet and warm, one might select an establishment tricked out with Neapolitan, National, or revolutionary flags, or a straw-festooned rustic stage set, or a white-clothed and black-tied mock-up of a baronial manse, or a dim long hall with red beveled globes that smoked as if underwater from atop the low tables. At the far wall of this latter establishment, set in a rocky crèche, was a tank deep with dark-to-bright green-blue tumescence, a shifting of sentient shells.

As one peered over a corridor of human shoulders into this magnetic trough, this glowing blue shifted onto a dashed armada of upraised mottled claws—blue, green, and brown—pinched together and bound shut with humiliatingly candy-colored rubber bindings. Swaths of bubbles drained palliatively down from an upright filter to cloak and disclose these contents at intervals, parting limply each time to reveal fat, listing armatures and, below them, their several creatures straining like so many smoking and encrusted brains to solve out this new knot of logic. For what stymied them now was not the depth their senses were developed for but the invisible, cold, hard material that held them in its rectangular grasp within the larger rectangular grasp of the room, and the plasmic sprawl of the city beyond it, and the husk of the catastrophic atmosphere beyond that. *Tap tap.*

At the glass.

The souls of blind folks.

That glass, so foreign, which was once so ironically seafloor or shore, now pressed and converted, would, across time, sink. Molt and remolt like the lobster's back. Mothermaterial itself upon which these creatures, heaped on one another, battled to exhaustion or were singled out by the vitality of their fighting to meet the heat of the pot. Hiss and blot. To be carried insensate across that boundary at last, in a matter of minutes, to the swish of the swinging door. To arrive at the guest's table with an offering of seawater still clutched in its claws.

For the one who comes in through the door is the Bridegroom.

Is this on? Am I live here? The room-hiss can be edited out, yes? The level brought down? The level brought up? The bed of silver and the bed of greens. The lemon slices with their eyes wide like wise children. That hold their own acidic wisdom in their gasp. Blind them, bind them in a sieving cloth and squeeze. What bitter tears lapse and relapse.

Citizens of Nation: Open your eyes. What do we look out or look in on, what is our portion. Listing and silting in the dwindling tub. The element itself sizzles and hisses. When we close our eyes we are bathed in trouble. When we reject the wisdom our senses are poised for. When we battle not in our own depth but in some flammable empyrean toxic to us. When we are brought into a rivalrous and deadly proximity yet cannot work together.

The glass is clear, or nearly so. Soon it will be so clear it will disappear.

A child says to you, what was the grass?

You may refer him to a full complement of vetted and approved instructional software packages: perspectives biological, ecological, Continental, Zen, Thomist, and Levantine. Stamped and saturated, the cardboard boxes gleam in their plastic sheathes, wisdom in a row of cupidy teeth. Even in my mind's eye I sigh to stand before it, an unspent gasp here wheezing from the folded plastic at but a finger's touch. It makes a tooth-grittingly beautiful music, how the transparent creaking folds meet and are sealed. Perfect model planet: a nail-thin, colorless crust; the dilating glossy laminate surface; the unseen layers of fiber; the pure molded plastic fissures and berths; and then the disks and chips that hold information laced upon itself and dreaming, cool and fetal and incubatory inside the zealous, faithful packaging.

It is a wondrous age we live in, and luckier than the events of E and Re-E day might cause us at first to conclude. Much—all—is unpredictable. The sky bruises and swells closed, or it gapes vacantly away as if searching for a window high in itself, there to gaze out onto other universes and away from our planet's pitted, pitiful face. We are re-pioneering in our own parched land, which was once our Eden. Which devolved from Eden to Nod and revolved to Eden many cyclical times in its own closed book of history. It versed and reversed itself. Now it seems to have ended. We are laid low, in the lowness of its motion. Pioneers of stasis. Nation spreads around us with all its vast immunity suppressed, its resources unable to regenerate themselves. A book, a husk of corn, a favorite shirt, the DNA of a clambering beetle—all is reduced to the same denatured dust now, golden and sere and the useless stuff of parable and paradox. The past is an object lesson tending to no point. We fumble to repurpose the materials still around us, concatenate an education software package here, a new formula for foodstuffs at the next lab down the road. We keep ourselves going, but not growing. Still the Nation. Still, the Nation, realtime model, quiet as a breeze, trace of three long vestigial carpals over the rockface of the fossil record.

Lest this seem a dismal vista, O, Pioneers, please look again. For how delicately and permanently we are poised. Gilded by the last light of the last era and lit with the anticipation of the next. We need do nothing but keep our balance. A knot, a bolus of events will certainly collect themselves and produce a future as if from their own material and push our society with it into a new epoch. Whether we find ourselves on a seafloor or a mountaintop on that day, we will be altogether reconstituted, yet continuous, our same particle-by-particle makeup of a species now winged, gilled, equipped for new etherea that will come with the new age.

For now, citizens, absorb. Convert and consume. Reprocess and engorge. Sufficiency in abundance. Be mindful. Think: cells. Sip this lucidity. Self-knowledge. It's the same all over. Couch-surf. Dip your ankles into the gentle swells. Be faithful to the interface. Attend it. Keep your loved ones close, and turn the faces of the youngest to this nutritious, mellifluous light.

What can be folded away:

Socks, charters, self.

The ridiculous and the sublime. Reticulated sports-dome and sublimated desire. Muscled limb and lethal jaw. The genetic ribbon and the deathless sentence. When we flew over the long-abandoned city, how that Capitol complex ached and dropped its panes. Shadow of the chopper like a dragonfly or toy rippled across the floodplain and the sepulchral stairs rising ceaselessly like a flood. From above, its round, degraded form resembled a crumpled face within a too-perfect, circular frame: victimhood, the human being without personality and thus at its most humane. And the floodplain was a dull mirror, reflecting only our insectoidal carriage in the dull and mirroring sky. What is personality but the inhuman layer, whether animaline or godly, or pathological—it must be shed like a virus. All must be degraded. Blessed similitude. The swept-clean face of the featureless landscape. The non-orientation of a calm, magnetized needle. The satisfied race. It consumes without hunger, is nourished and survives. Is nourished and replaced.

RETRIEVAL DREAM

It can be done: retrieval dream. Because stasis works backwards as well as forwards. Because it doesn't work at all. Knife the bivalve. Drive the steam. Force the lock. Lift the river. Sieve the despot. Denature the logic. Return the money. Reduce to its elements. Stir. Even in the basest car ads, the wheels appear to spin backwards. Is it so hard to imagine, then, the safe route out of our current predicament? I am referring to the whole race lost and predacious as in a cavern/ in a canyon. That is the true subtext of our Marianne's, the girl's, Flet's, Clementine's death in a sere arroyo. Garroted not drowned. Begotten not made. Choked on a slim concertina of dust and faith.

How that wire, deployed, may constrict. May contract. May withdraw, and in withdrawing expand, and grow more deadly. Bisonorous, arranged in histrionic patterns, it provides a temporary obstruction, growing less temporary by the day—less temporary as it gets more involved in time. The soldiers erect one-and-a-half kilometers per hour, a dancing maze that eventually hems them in. The devils bring it all to disorder in a night's width, and the dunes disarrange and shift places. The whole flyspecked proceeding flashes like a cirrus cloud—like both the horse and its whip. And its urging. And its speed.

But how will the goods reach the people now? The MachSix razors, the Minute-Gourmets and -Maids? Suspended like harps in a tree, like hearths, hunger delusions, suspended like burning wreaths, strange fruit, a tarred and breakneck angle, flightless bird, tarry, tarry night. The brilliant bicameral eyes and minds and the sightless tracker dogs. All work in concert. Concertina! And there is the maestro now, and there is the Master, I can see it all from my place in the tree.

I am the star that completes the crèche. O wanderer, follow me. I'm threading a hole in the sky, a saucy keyhole, I'm thrumming the Babe with my tippy-toe. See how It glares from Its place in the manger. See how Its cradle cap flares.

To reach through the glass to the room's reflection is to reach out of the room. To break the pane of belief with a blang and drum corp. And clams casino. And a clang and droll club. Those ham sandwiches look good enough to eat, posed like their likeness amid reels of waxen fruit. That fruit looks good enough to cast on the waters; it'd float right back to thee. Salty, juicen fruit. To lift the fish-flesh with the brilliant tine, to lift the fish eye out of the floodtide so that it may address the faithful is to denude the sea. Nude and deluded I was faced with my weakness and it all looked weak to me. Bravo. A well-timed concession. Now slick back down to your lick of sea. To your broadcast channel. To your manifest network. In time to be received, nonidentically. To be reconsumed, retrieved.

I write this, I utter it, I think it, which is to say I do not utter it at all, which is to say not say it. Anything. Literally, quite utterly. No. Molecules cluster the room calmly, attend each other with quiet ministrations, admixture of my own effluvia, some titrate of atmosphere, and the room's material prerogatives, husking, decomposing, more than dense enough to clasp and buffer whatever thought should also ray out into it. How the miniclimate so lovingly preserves this cone of light cast from the metal brainpan that shields the aging bulb, one of a crate of hundreds also aging, their filaments dried as the species of another century, in a corner of the room. The bulbs hold also intelligence, lightweight with the weight of light, which is time divided. Force is elsewhere. The cone casts a dry and perfect circle onto my desk-face, onto paper grainy as a visage, a back of the hand, a head turned away. The closer one looks it is more and more whorled with grain. More and more riven. Featureless and already a map. The sheet, too, has brothers, duplicates, a whisper-thin army and array. More and more time I spend here in the closed room fit to this cone of light, with my tumbler at the ready, and in my hand another glass, for magnifying, and my kit for marking and measuring laid aside, the compass and the protractor cool and metallic, the pencil dry as if it had never known my grasp.

More and more time.

Cross the room to a glossed plate glass that exists only in memory. Who is in the window as in a shudder of waves. As in a waiver of water. As in a file fat with a corpuscular brief. Who is fish-mouthed and preserved. Face drained to the very lips. There, oxygen bursting in the pant of blood. Rusting on the inside. Who mouths these words over shoulder and collar. My mouth at various ages. My smile thinning or full or bottle-mouthing in agreeance or amazement. The brown, slicked-down hair of my disposition. The unflagging wave of graves. Unfurling, filamental surveyors. Follicles palpating the underground. Can dead cells be sentimental. They hold data can they read it. Can they grow through data and take the shape of its dots and dashes, its naughts and strokes. Information keystrokes, striating the earth like muscle. Muscular seizure, dried, scraping chemical seas.

Alchemical notion: Transform me beyond the human. Regress me out of information, carry me past the knowledge banks. Pure data and its opposite alleles shift and contradict, harmonize, nothing so narrow as history, rays in all direction, wave and thread, nodeless. A mapless non-system infinite and infinitesimal, choiceless and without scale.

The antique questions: How many universes on the graphite tip of this geometer's stylus and how many in each eye-socket in the sleepless wreck and how many in each rung of the ancient astrolabe rotting out of view. Beneath the degrading water. Vision of stars and earthly celestial city of subatomic particles, coifed cumuli and whipped ziggurat whirring and shattering out of view.

No verses. No vision and no view.

Swirl the tumbler. Marl-eye, whiskey knuckler. Withdraw. Sink and swoon into the stalwart chair that holds me in an attitude of alertness. Rest in the here-'n-now. Swept up, slept.

FENCE BOOKS

THE MOTHERWELL PRIZE

Unspoiled Air	Kaisa Ullsrik Miller

THE ALBERTA PRIZE

The Cow	Ariana Reines
Practice, Restraint	Laura Sims
A Magic Book	Sasha Steensen
Sky Girl	Rosemary Griggs
The Real Moon of Poetry and Other Poems	Tina Brown Celona
Zirconia	Chelsey Minnis

FENCE MODERN POETS SERIES

Structure of the Embryonic Rat Brain	Christopher Janke
The Stupefying Flashbulbs	Daniel Brenner
Povel	Geraldine Kim
The Opening Question	Prageeta Sharma
Apprehend	Elizabeth Robinson
The Red Bird	Joyelle McSweeney

ANTHOLOGIES & CRITICAL WORKS

Not for Mothers Only: Contemporary Poets on Child-Getting & Child-Rearing
Catherine Wagner & Rebecca Wolff, editors

FREE CHOICE POETRY

Bad Bad	Chelsey Minnis
Snip Snip!	Tina Brown Celona
Yes, Master	Michael Earl Craig
Swallows	Martin Corless-Smith
Folding Ruler Star	Aaron Kunin
The Commandrine and Other Poems	Joyelle McSweeney
Macular Hole	Catherine Wagner
Nota	Martin Corless-Smith
Father of Noise	Anthony McCann
Can You Relax in My House	Michael Earl Craig
Miss America	Catherine Wagner

FREE CHOICE FICTION

Flet: A Novel	Joyelle McSweeney
The Mandarin	Aaron Kunin

Fence Books is an extension of **FENCE**, a biannual journal of poetry, fiction, art, and criticism that has a mission to redefine the terms of accessibility by publishing challenging writing distinguished by idiosyncrasy and intelligence rather than by allegiance with camps, schools, or cliques. It is part of our press's mission to support writers who might otherwise have difficulty being recognized because their work doesn't answer to either the mainstream or to recognizable modes of experimentation.

The Motherwell Prize is an annual series, generously endowed by Jennifer S. Epstein, which offers publication of a first or second book of poems by a woman, as well as a five thousand dollar cash prize.

Our second prize series is the Fence Modern Poets Series. This contest is open to poets of any gender and at any stage of career, and offers a one thousand dollar cash prize in addition to book publication.

For more information about either prize, visit www.fencebooks.com, or send an SASE to: Fence Books/[Name of Prize], New Library 320, University at Albany, 1400 Washington Avenue, Albany, NY, 12222.

For more about **FENCE**, visit www.fencemag.com.